The Lord of Death and the Queen of Life

Homer Eon Flint

THE LORD OF DEATH AND THE QUEEN OF LIFE

Originally published in *Argosy-All Story Weekly,*
May 1919, and August 1919.

ISBN 13: 978-1-4344-8502-1

THE LORD OF DEATH

PART I

THE DISCOVERY

I

THE SKY CUBE

THE DOCTOR, who was easily the most musical
of the four men, sang in a cheerful baritone:

"The owl and the pussy-cat went to sea
In a beautiful, pea-green boat."

The geologist, who had held down the lower end of a
quartet in his university days, growled an accompaniment
under his breath as he blithely peeled the potatoes. Occasionally a high-pitched note or two came from the direction
of the engineer; he could not spare much wind while clam-
bering about the machinery, oil-can in hand. The architect,
alone, ignored the famous tune.

"What I can't understand, Smith," he insisted, "is how you draw the electricity from the ether into this car without blasting us all to cinders."

The engineer squinted through an opal glass shutter into one of the tunnels, through which the anti-gravitation current was pouring. "If you didn't know any more about buildings than you do about machinery, Jackson," he grunted, because of his squatting position, "I'd hate to live in one of your houses!"

The architect smiled grimly. "You're living in one of 'em right now, Smith," said he; "that is, if you call this car a house."

Smith straightened up. He was an unimportant-looking man, of medium height and build, and bearing a mild, good-humored expression. Nobody would ever look at him twice, would ever guess that his skull concealed an unusually complete knowledge of electricity, mechanisms, and such practical matters.

"I told you yesterday, Jackson," he said, "that the air surrounding the earth is chock full of electricity. And—"

"And that the higher we go, the more juice," added the other, remembering. "As much as to say that it is the atmosphere, then, that protects the earth from the surrounding voltage."

The engineer nodded. "Occasionally it breaks through, anyhow, in the form of lightning. Now, in order to control that current, and prevent it from turning this machine, and us, into ashes, all we do is to pass the juice through a cylinder of highly compressed air, fixed in this wall. By varying the pressure and dampness within the cylinder, we can regulate the flow."

The builder nodded rapidly. "All right. But why doesn't the electricity affect the walls themselves? I thought they were made of steel."

The engineer glanced through the dead-light at the reddish disk of the Earth, hazy and indistinct at a distance of forty million miles. "It isn't steel; it's a non-magnetic alloy. Besides, there's a layer of crystalline sulphur between the alloy and the vacuum space."

"The vacuum is what keeps out the cold, isn't it?" Jackson knew, but he asked in order to learn more.

"Keeps out the sun's heat, too. The outer shell is pretty blamed hot on that side, just as hot as it is cold on the shady side." Smith seated himself beside a huge electrical machine, a rotary converter which he next indicated with a jerk of his thumb. "But you don't want to forget that the juice outside is no use to us, the way it is. We have to change it.

"It's neither positive nor negative; it's just neutral. So we separate it into two parts; and all we have to do, when we want to get away from the earth or any other magnetic-sphere, is to aim a bunch of positive current at the corresponding pole of the planet, or negative current at the other pole. Like poles repel, you know."

"Listens easy," commented Jackson. "Too easy."

"Well, it isn't exactly as simple as all that. Takes a lot of apparatus, all told," and the engineer looked about the room, his glance resting fondly on his beloved machinery.

The big room, fifty feet square, was almost filled with machines; some reached nearly to the ceiling, the same distance above. In fact, the interior of the "cube," as that form of sky-car was known, had very little waste space. The living quarters of the four men who occupied it had to be fitted in wherever there happened to be room. The architect's own berth was sandwiched in between two huge dynamos.

He was thinking hard. "I see now why you have such a lot of adjustments for those tunnels," meaning the six square tubes which opened into the ether through the six walls of the room. "You've got to point the juice pretty accurately."

"I should say so." Smith led the way to a window, and the two shaded their eyes from the lights within while they gazed at the ashy glow of Mercury, toward which they were traveling. "I've got to adjust the current so as to point exactly toward his northern half." Smith might have added that a continual stream of repelling current was still directed to-

ward the earth, and another toward the sun, away over to
their right; both to prevent being drawn off their course.

"And how fast are we going?"

"Four or five times as fast as mother earth: between eighty
and ninety miles per second. It's easy to get up speed out
here, of course, where there's no air resistance."

Another voice broke in. The geologist had finished his potatoes, and a savory smell was already issuing from the frying
pan. Years spent in the wilderness had made the geologist
a good cook, and doubly welcome as a member of the expedition.

"We ought to get there tomorrow, then," he said eagerly.
Indoor life did not appeal to him, even under such exciting
circumstances. He peered at Mercury through his binoculars.
"Beginning to show up fine now."

The builder improved upon Van Emmon's example by
setting up the car's biggest telescope, a four-inch tube of
unusual excellence. All three pronounced the planet, which
was three-fourths "full" as they viewed it, as having pretty
much the appearance of the moon.

"Wonder why there's always been so much mystery about
Mercury?" pondered the architect invitingly. "Looks as though
the big five-foot telescope on Mt. Wilson would have shown
everything."

"Ask doc," suggested Smith, diplomatically. Jackson turned
and hailed the little man on the other side of the car. He
looked up absently from the scientific apparatus with which
he had been making a test of the room's chemically purified
air, then he stepped to the oxygen tanks and closed the
flow a trifle, referring to his figures in the severely exact
manner of his craft. He crossed to the group.

"Mercury is so close to the sun," he answered the architect's question, "he's always been hard to observe. For a long
time the astronomers couldn't even agree that he always keeps
the same face toward the sun, like the moon toward the
earth."

"Then his day is as long as his year?"

"Eighty-eight of our days; yes."

THE LORD OF DEATH

"Continual sunlight! He can't be inhabited, then?" The architect knew very little about the planets. He had been included in the party because, along with his professional knowledge, he possessed remarkable ability as an amateur antiquarian. He knew as much about the doings of the ancients as the average man knows of baseball.

Dr. Kinney shook his head. "Not at present, certainly."

Instantly Jackson was alert. "Then perhaps there were people there at one time!"

"Why not?" the doctor put it lightly. "There's little or no atmosphere there now, of course, but that's not saying there never has been. Even if he is such a little planet—less than three thousand, smaller than the moon—he must have had plenty of air and water at one time, the same as the Earth."

"What's become of the air?" Van Emmon wanted to know. Kinney eyed him in reproach. He said:

"You ought to know. Mercury has only two-fifths as much gravitation as the earth; a man weighing a hundred and fifty back home would be only a sixty-pounder there. And you can't expect stuff as light as air to stay forever on a planet with no more pull than that, when the sun is on the job only thirty-six millions miles away."

"About a third as far as from the Earth to the sun," commented the engineer. "By George, it must be hot!"

"On the sunlit side, yes," said Kinney. "On the dark side it is as cold as space itself—four hundred and sixty below, Fahrenheit."

They considered this in silence for some minutes. The builder went to another window and looked at Venus, at that time about sixty million miles distant, on the far side of the sun. They were intending to visit "Earth's twin sister" on their return. After a while he came back to the group, ready with another question:

"If Mercury ever was inhabited, then his day wasn't as long as it is now, was it?"

"No," said the doctor. "In all probability he once had a day the same length as ours. Mercury is a comparatively old

9

planet, you know; being smaller, he cooled off earlier than the earth, and has been more affected by the pull of the sun. But it's been a mighty long time since he had a day like ours; before the earth was cool enough to live on, probably."

"But since Mercury was made out of the same batch of material—" prompted the geologist.

"No reason, then, why life shouldn't have existed there in the past!" exclaimed the architect, his eyes sparkling with the instinct of the born antiquarian. He glanced up eagerly as the doctor coughed apologetically and said:

"Don't forget that, even if Mercury is part baked and part frozen, there must be a region in between which is neither." He picked up a small globe from the table and ran a finger completely around it from pole to pole. "So. There must be a narrow band of country where the sun is only partly above the horizon, and where the climate is temperate."

"Then"—the architect almost shouted in his excitement, an excitement only slightly greater than that of the other two—"then, if there were people on Mercury at one time—"

The doctor nodded gravely. "There may be some there now!"

II

A DEAD CITY

FROM A HEIGHT of a few thousand miles Mercury, at first glance, strongly reminded them of the moon. The general effect was the same—leaden disk, with slight prominences here and there on the circumference, and large, irregular splotches of a darkish shade relieved by a great many brilliantly lighted areas, lines, and spots.

A second glance, however, found a marked difference. Instead of the craters, which always distinguished the moon, Mercury showed ranges of bona fide mountains.

The doctor gave a sigh of regret, mixed with a generous amount of excitement. "Too bad those mountains weren't distinguishable from the earth," he complained. "We wouldn't have been so quick to brand Mercury a dead world."

The others were too engrossed to comment. The sky-car was rapidly sinking nearer and nearer the planet; already Smith had stopped the current with which he had attracted the cube toward the little world's northern hemisphere, and was now using negative voltage. This, in order to act as a brake, and prevent them from falling to destruction.

Suddenly Van Emmon, the geologist, whose eyes had been glued to his binoculars, gave an exclamation of wonder. "Look at those faults!" He pointed toward a region south of that for which they were bound; what might be called the planet's torrid zone.

At first it was hard to see; then, little by little, there unfolded before their eyes a giant, spiderlike system of chasms in the strange surface beneath them. From a point almost directly opposite the sun, these cracks radiated in a half-dozen different directions; vast, irregular clefts, they ran through mountain and plain alike. In places they must have been hundreds of miles wide, while there was no guessing as to their depth. For all that the four in the cube could see, they were bottomless.

"Small likelihood of anybody being alive there now," commented the geologist skeptically. "If the sun has dried it out enough to produce faults like that, how could animal life exist?"

"Notice, however," prompted the doctor, "that the cracks do not extend all the way to the edge of the disk." This was true; all the great chasms ended far short of the "twilight band" which the doctor had declared might still contain life.

But as the sky-car rushed downward their attention became fixed upon the surface directly beneath them, a point whose latitude corresponded roughly with that of New York on the Earth. It was a region of low-lying mountains, decidedly different from various precipitous ranges to be seen to the north and east. On the west, or left-hand side of this district, a comparatively level stretch, with an occasional

11

peak or two projecting, suggested the ancient bed of an ocean.

By this time they were within a thousand miles. Smith threw on a little more current; their speed diminished to a safer point, and they scanned the approaching surface with the greatest of care. The architect, who was a New Yorker, was strongly reminded of the fall aspect of the Appalachians; but Van Emmon, who was born and raised on the Pacific coast, declared that the spot was almost exactly like the region north of San Francisco. "If I didn't know where I was," he declared, "I'd be trying to locate Eureka right now."

The engineer smiled tolerantly. He had spent several years in Scotland, and he felt sure, he obligingly told the others, that this new locality was far more like the Ben Lomond country than any other spot on earth. He was so positive, he made the doctor, a New Zealander, smile quite broadly.

"It is just like the hills near my home," he stated, with an air of finality which made further discussion useless.

"There's a river!" the architect suddenly exclaimed, pointing; then added, before the others could comment, "I mean, what was once a river." They saw that he was right; an irregular but well-defined streak of sandy hue trickled down the middle of their chosen destination—a long, L-shaped valley, surrounded by low hills.

"That's the most likely place, outside of the twilight zone, for life to be found," remarked the doctor. "Neither mountainous nor dead level."

He added: "The spectroscope has plainly shown that there's water vapor in what little air there is. Must be precious little. If the air was as humid as the earth's, we couldn't see the surface at all from this height."

The inviting-looking valley was now less than a hundred miles below. Inviting, however, only in outline; in color it was a grayish buff, scorched and forbidding. The hills were yellower, and an alkali white on their summits.

"Do either of you fellows see anything *green?*" demanded the engineer, a little later. They were silent; each had noticed long before, that not even near the poles was there the slightest sign of vegetation.

"No chance unless there's foliage," muttered the doctor, half to himself. The builder asked what he meant. He explained: "So far as we know, all animal life depends upon vegetation for its oxygen. Not only the oxygen in the air, but that stored in the plants which animals eat. Unless there's greenery—"

He paused at a low exclamation from Smith. The engineer's eyes were fixed, in wonder and excitement, upon that part of the valley which lay at the joint of the "L" below them. It was perhaps six miles across; and all over the comparatively smooth surface jutted dark projections. Viewed through the glasses, they had a regular, uniform appearance.

"By Jove!" ejaculated the doctor, almost in awe. He leaned forward and scrubbed the dead-light for the tenth time. All four men strained their eyes to see.

It was the architect who broke the silence which followed. The other three were content to let the thrill of the thing have its way with them. Such a feeling had little weight with the expert in archeology.

"Well," he declared jubilantly in his boyish voice, "either I eat my hat or that's a genuine, bona fide city!"

As swiftly as an elevator drops, and as safely, the cube shot straight downward. Every second the landscape narrowed and shrunk, leaving the remaining details larger, clearer, sharper. Bit by bit the amazing thing below them resolved itself into a real metropolis.

Within five minutes they were less than a mile above it. Smith threw on more current, so that the descent stopped; and the cube hung motionless in space.

For another five minutes the four men studied the scene in nervous silence. Each knew that the others were looking for the same thing—some sign of life. A little spot of green, or possibly something in motion—a single whiff of smoke would have been enough to cause a whoop of joy.

But nobody shouted. There was nothing to shout about.

Nowhere in all that locality apparently was there the slightest indication that any save themselves were alive.

Instead, the most extraordinary city that man had ever laid eyes upon was stretched directly beneath. It was grouped about what seemed to be the meeting-point of three great roads, which led to this spot from as many passes through the surrounding hills. And the city seemed thus naturally divided into three segments, of equal size and shape, and each with its own street system.

For they undoubtedly were streets. No metropolis on earth ever had its blocks laid out with such unvarying exactness. This Mercurian city contained none but perfect equilateral triangles, and the streets themselves were of absolutely uniform width.

The buildings, however, showed no such uniformity. On the outskirts of this brilliantly tan mystery the blocks seemed to contain nothing save odd heaps of dingy, sun-baked mud. On the extreme north, however, lay five blocks grouped together, whose buildings, like those in the middle of the city, were rather tall, square-cut and of the same dusty, cream-white hue.

"Down-town" were several structures especially prominent for their height. They towered to such an extent, in fact, that their upper windows were easily made out. Apparently they were hundreds of stories high!

Here and there on the streets could be seen small spots, colored a darker buff than the rest of that dazzling landscape. But not one of the spots was moving.

"We'll go down further," said the engineer tentatively, in a low tone. There was no comment. He gradually reduced the repelling current, so that the sky-car resumed its descent.

They sank down until they were on a level with the top of one of those extraordinary sky-scrapers. The roof seemed perfectly flat, except for a large, round, black opening in its center. No one was in sight.

When opposite the upper row of windows, at a distance of perhaps twenty feet, Smith brought the car to a halt, and

14

they peered in. There were no panes; the windows opened directly into a vast room; but nothing was clearly visible in the blackness save the outlines of the opening in the opposite walls.

They went down further, keeping well to the middle of the space above the street. At every other yard they kept a sharp lookout for the inhabitants; but so far as they could see, their approach was entirely unobserved.

When within fifty yards of the surface, all four men made a search for cross-wires below. They saw none; there were no poles, even. Neither, to their astonishment, was there such a thing as a sidewalk. The street stretched, unbroken by curbing, from wall to wall and from corner to corner.

As the cube settled slowly to the ground, the adventurers left the deadlight to use the windows. For a moment the view was obscured by a swirl of dust, raised by the spurt of the current; then this cloud vanished, settling to the ground with astounding suddenness, as though jerked down by some invisible hand.

Directly ahead of them, distant perhaps a hundred yards, lay a yellowish-brown mass of unusual octagonal shape. One end contained a small oval opening, but the men from the Earth looked in vain for any creature to emerge from it.

The doctor silently set to work with his apparatus. From an air-tight double-doored compartment he obtained a sample of the ether outside the car; and with the aid of previously arranged chemicals, quickly learned the truth.

There was no air. Not only was there no oxygen, the element upon which all known life depends, but there was no nitrogen, no carbon dioxide; not the slightest trace of water vapor or of the other less known elements which can be found in small amounts in our own atmosphere. Clearly, as the doctor said, whatever air the astronomers had observed must exist on the circumference of the planet only, and not in this sun-blasted, north-central spot.

On the outer walls of the cube, so arranged as to be visible through the windows, were various instruments. The bar-

15

ometer showed no pressure. The thermometer, a specially devised one which used gas instead of mercury, showed a temperature of six hundred degrees, Fahrenheit.

No air, no water, and a baking heat; as the geologist remarked, how could life exist there? But the architect suggested that possibly there was some form of life, of which men knew nothing, which could exist under such circumstances.

They got out three of the suits. These were a good deal like those worn by divers, except that the outer layer was made of non-conducting aluminum cloth, flexible, air-tight, and strong. Between it and the inner lining was a layer of cells, into which the men now pumped several pints of liquid oxygen. The terrific cold of this chemical made the heavy flannel of the inner lining very welcome; while the oxygen itself, as fast as it evaporated, revitalized the air within the big, glass-faced helmet.

Once safely locked within the clumsy suits, Jackson, Van Emmon, and Smith took their places within the vestibule; while the doctor, who had volunteered to stay behind, watched them open the outer door. With a hiss all the air in the vestibule rushed out; and the doctor earnestly thanked his stars that the inner door had been built very strongly.

The men stepped out on to the ground. At first they moved with great care, being uncertain that their feet were weighted heavily enough to counteract the reduced gravitation of the tiny planet. But they had been living in a very peculiar condition, gravitationally speaking, for the past three days; and they quickly adapted themselves. After a little shifting about, the three artificial monsters gave their telephone wires another scrutiny; then, keeping always within ten feet of each other, so as not to throw any strain on the connections, they strode in a matter-of-fact way toward the nearest doorway.

For a moment or two they stood outside the queer, peaked archway, their glimmering suits standing out oddly in the blinding sunlight. Then they advanced boldly into the

16

opening; in a flash they vanished from the doctor's sight, and the inklike blackness of the opening again stared at him from that dazzling wall.

III

THE HOUSE OF DUST

THE GEOLOGIST, strong man that he was, and by profession an investigator of the unknown—Van Emmon—took the lead. He stalked straight ahead into a vast space which, without any preliminary hallway, filled the entire triangular block.

Before their eyes were accustomed to the shadow—"Pretty cold," murmured the architect into the phone transmitter; it was fastened to the inside of the helmet, directly in front of his mouth, while the receiver was placed beside his ear. All three stopped short to adjust each other's electrical heating apparatus. To do this, they did not use their fingers directly; they manipulated ingenious non-magnetic pliers attached to the ends of fingerless, insulated mittens.

Before they had finished, the builder, who had been puzzling over the extraordinary suddenness with which that cloud of dust had settled, received an inspiration. He was carrying note-book and camera. With his pliers he tore out a sheet from the former, and holding book in one hand and the leaf in the other, he allowed them to drop at the same instant.

They reached the ground together.

"See?" The architect repeated the experiment. "Back home, where there's air, the paper would have floated down; it would have taken three times as long for it to fall as the book."

Smith nodded, but he had been thinking of something else. He said gravely: "Remember what I told you—it's air that insulates the earth from the ether. If there's no air here" —he glanced out into the pitiless sunlight—"then I hope there's no flaw in our insulation. We're walking in an electrical bath."

They looked around. Objects were pretty distinct now. They could easily see that the floor was covered with what appeared to be machines, laid out in orderly fashion. Here, however, as outside, everything was coated with that fine, cream-colored dust. It filled every nook and cranny; it stirred about their feet with every step.

The geologist led the way down a broad aisle, on either side of which towered immense machinery. Smith was for stopping to examine them one by one; but the others vetoed the engineer's passion, and strode on toward the end of the triangle. More than anything else, they looked for the absent population to show itself.

Suddenly Van Emmon stopped short. "Is it possible that they're all asleep?" He added that, even though the sun shone steadily the year around, the people must take time for rest.

But Smith stirred the dust with his foot and shook his head. "I've seen no tracks. This dust has been lying here for weeks, perhaps months. If the folks are away, then they must be taking a community vacation."

At the end of the aisle they reached a small, railed-in space, strongly resembling what might be seen in any office on the earth. In the middle of it stood a low, flat-topped desk, for all the world like that of a prosperous real-estate agent, except that it was about half a foot lower. There was no chair. For lack of a visible gate in the railing, the explorers stepped over, being careful not to touch it.

There was nothing on top of the desk save the usual coat of dust. Below, a very wide space had been left for the legs of whoever had used it; and flanking this space were two pedestals, containing what looked to be a multitude of exceedingly small drawers. Smith bent and examined them; apparently they had no locks; and he unhesitatingly reached out, gripped the knob of one and pulled.

Noiselessly, instantaneously, the whole desk crumbled to powder.

THE LORD OF DEATH

Startled, Smith stumbled backwards, knocking against the railing. Next instant it lay on the floor, its fragments scarcely distinguishable from what had already covered the surface. Only a tiny cloud of dust arose, and in half a second this had settled.

The three looked at each other significantly. Clearly, the thing that had just happened argued a great lapse of time since the user of that desk officiated in that enclosure. It looked as though Smith's guess of "weeks, perhaps months," would have to be changed to years, perhaps centuries.

"Feel all right?" asked the geologist. Jackson and Smith made affirmative noises; and again they stepped out, this time walking in the aisle along the outer wall. They could see their sky-car plainly through the ovals.

Here the machinery could be examined more closely. They resembled automatic testing scales, said Smith; such as is used in weighing complicated metal products after finishing and assembling. Moreover, they seemed to be connected, the one to the other, with a series of endless belts, which Smith thought indicated automatic production. To all appearances, the dust-covered apparatus stood just as it had been left when operations ceased, an unguessable length of time before.

Smith showed no desire to touch the things now. Seeing this, the geologist deliberately reached out and scraped the dust from the nearest machine; and to the vast relief of all three, no damage was done. The dust fell straight to the floor, exposing a brilliantly polished streak of greenish-white metal.

Van Emmon made another tentative brush or so at other points, with the same result. Clean, untarnished metal lay beneath all that dust. Clearly it was some non-conducting alloy; whatever it was, it had successfully resisted the action of the elements all the while that such presumably wooden articles as the desk and railing had been steadily rotting.

Emboldened, Smith clambered up on the frame of one of the machines. He examined it closely as to its cams, clutches, gearing, and other details significant enough to his mechanical training. He noted their adjustments, scrutinized the con-

19

veying apparatus, and came back carrying a cylindrical object which he had removed from an automatic chuck.

"This is what they were making," he remarked, trying to conceal his excitement. The others brushed the dust from the thing, a huge piece of metal which would have been too much for their strength on the earth. Instantly they identified it.

It was a cannon shell.

Again Van Emmon led the way. They took a reassuring glance out the window at the familiar cube, then passed along the aisle toward the farther corner. As they neared it they saw that it contained a small enclosure of heavy metal scrollwork, within which stood a triangular elevator.

The men examined it as closely as possible, noting especially the extremely low stool which stood upon its platform. The same unerodable metal seemed to have been used throughout the whole affair.

After a careful scrutiny of the two levers which appeared to control the thing—"I'm going to try it out," announced Smith, well knowing that the others would have to go with him if they kept the telephones intact. They protested that the thing was not safe; Smith replied that they had seen no stairway, or anything corresponding to one. "If this lift is made of that alloy," admiringly, "then it's safe." But Jackson managed to talk him out of it.

When they returned to the heap of powdered wood which had been the desk, Smith spied a long work-bench under a nearby window. There they found a very ordinary vise, in which was clamped a piece of metal; but for the dust, it might have been placed there ten minutes before. On the bench lay several tools, some familiar to the engineer and some entirely strange. A set of screw-drivers of various sizes caught his eye. He picked them up, and again experienced the sensation of having wood turn to dust at his touch. The blades were whole.

Still searching, the engineer found a square metal chest of drawers, each of which he promptly opened. The contents were laden with dust, but he brushed this off and disclosed a quantity of exceedingly delicate instruments. They were more like dentists' tools than machinists', yet plainly were intended for mechanical use.

One drawer held what appeared to be a roll of drawings. Smith did not want to touch them; with infinite care he blew off the dust with the aid of his oxygen pipe. After a moment or two the surface was clear, but it offered no encouragement; it was the blank side of the paper.

There was no help for it. Smith grasped the roll firmly with his pliers—and next second gazed upon dust.

In the bottom drawer lay something that aroused the curiosity of all three. These were small reels, about two inches in diameter and a quarter of an inch thick, each incased in a tight-fitting box. They resembled measuring tapes to some extent, except that the ribbons were made of marvelously thin material. Van Emmon guessed that there were a hundred yards in a roll. Smith estimated it at three hundred. They seemed to be made of a metal similar to that composing the machines. Smith pocketed them all.

It was the builder who thought to look under the bench, but it was Smith who had brought a light. By its aid they discovered a very small machine, decidedly like a stock ticker, except that it had no glass dome, but possessed at one end a curious metal disk about a foot in diameter. Apparently it had been undergoing repairs; it was impossible to guess its purpose. Smith's pride was instantly aroused; he tucked it under his arm, and was impatient to get back to the cube, where he might more carefully examine his find with the tips of his fingers.

It was when they were about to leave the building that they thought to inspect walls and ceiling. Not that anything worth while was to be seen; the surfaces seemed perfectly plain and bare, except for the inevitable dust. Even the uppermost corners, ten feet above their heads, showed dust to the light of Smith's electric torch.

Van Emmon stopped and stared at the spot as though fascinated. The others were ready to go; they turned and looked at him curiously. For a moment or two he seemed struggling for breath.

"Good Heavens!" he gasped, almost in a whisper. His face was white; the other two leaped toward him, fearful that he was suffocating. But he pushed them away roughly.

"We're fools! Blind, blithering idiots—that's what we are!" He pointed toward the ceiling with a hand that trembled plainly, and went on in a voice which he tried to make fierce despite the awe which shook it.

"Look at that dust again! How'd it get there?" He paused while the others, the thought finally getting to them, felt a queer chill striking at the backs of their necks. "Men—there's only one way for the dust to settle on a wall! It's got to have air to carry it! It couldn't possibly get there without air!

"That dust settled long before life appeared on the Earth, even! It's been there ever since the air disappeared from Mercury!"

IV

THE LIBRARY

"I THOUGHT you'd never get back," complained the doctor crossly, when the three entered. They had been gone just half an hour.

Next moment he was studying their faces, and at once he demanded the most important fact. They told him, and before they had finished he was half-way into another suit. He was all eagerness; but somehow the three were very glad to be inside the cube again, and firmly insisted upon moving to another spot before making further explorations.

Within a minute or two the cube was hovering opposite the upper floor of the building the three had entered; and with only a foot of space separating the window of the sky-car and the dust-covered wall, the men from the earth inspected the interior at considerable length. They flashed a search-light all about the place, and concluded that it was the receiving-room, where the raw iron billets were brought via the elevator, and from there slid to the floor below. At one end, in exactly the same location as the desk Smith had destroyed, stood another, with a low and remarkably broad chair beside it.

So far as could be seen, there were neither doors, window-panes, nor shutters through the structure. "To get all the light and air they could," guessed the doctor. "Perhaps that's why the buildings are all triangular; most wall surface in proportion to floor area, that way."

A few hundred feet higher they began to look for promi-nent buildings. Only in forgetful moments did either of them scan the landscape for signs of life; they knew now that there could be none.

"We ought to learn something there," the doctor said after a while, pointing out a particularly large, squat, irregu-larly built affair on the edge of the "business district." The architect, however, was in favor of an exceptionally large, high building in the isolated group previously noted in the "suburbs." But because it was nearer, they maneuvered first in the direction of the doctor's choice.

The sky-car came to rest in a large plaza opposite what appeared to be the structure's main entrance. From their window the explorers saw that the squat effect was due only to the space the edifice covered; for it was an edifice, a full five stories high.

The doctor was impatient to go. Smith was willing enough to stay behind; he was already joyously examining the strange machine he had found. Two minutes later Kinney, Van Em-mon, and Jackson were standing before the portals of the great building.

There they halted, and no wonder. The entire face of the building could now be seen to be covered with a mass of carvings; for the most part they were statues in bas relief. All were fantastic in the extreme, but whether purposely so or not, there was no way to tell. Certainly any such work on the part of an earthly artist would have branded him either as insane or as an incomprehensible genius.

Directly above the entrance was a group which might have been labeled, "The Triumph of the Brute." An enormously powerful man, nearly as broad as he was tall, stood exulting over his victim, a less robust figure, prostrate under his feet. Both were clad in armor. The victor's face was distorted into a savage snarl, startlingly hideous by reason of the prodigious size of his head, planted as it was directly upon his shoulders; for he had no neck. His eyes were set so close together that at first glance they seemed to be but one. His nose was flat and African in type, while his mouth, devoid of curves, was simply revolting in its huge, thick-lipped lack of proportion. His chin was square and aggressive; his forehead, strangely enough, extremely high and narrow, rather than low and broad.

His victim lay in an attitude that indicated the most agonizing torture; his head was bent completely back, and around behind his shoulders. On the ground lay two battle-axes, huge affairs almost as heavy as the massively muscled men who had used them.

But the eyes of the explorers kept coming back to the fearsome face of the conqueror. From the brows down, he was simply a huge, brutal giant; above his eyes, he was an intellectual. The combination was absolutely frightful; the beast looked capable of anything, of overcoming any obstacle, mental or physical, internal or external, in order to assert his apparently enormous will. He could control himself or dominate others with equal ease and assurance.

"It can't be that he was drawn from life," said the doctor, with an effort. It wasn't easy to criticize that figure, lifeless though it was. "On a planet like this, with such slight gravitation, there is no need for such huge strength. The typical Mercurian should be tall and flimsy in build, rather than short and compact."

But the geologist differed. "We want to remember that the earth has no standard type. Think what a difference there is between the mosquito and the elephant, the snake and the

24

spider! One would suppose that they had been developed under totally different planetary conditions, instead of all right on the same globe.

"No; I think this monster may have been genuine." And with that the geologist turned to examine the other statuary.

Without exception, it resembled the central group; all the figures were neckless, and all much more heavily built than any people on earth. There were several female figures; they had the same general build, and in every case were so placed as to enhance the glory of the males. In one group the woman was offering up food and drink to a resting worker; in another she was being carried off, struggling, in the arms of a fairly good-looking warrior.

Dr. Kinney led the way into the building. As in the other structure, there was no door. The space seemed to be but one story in height, although that had the effect of a cathedral. The whole of the ceiling, irregularly arched in a curious, pointed manner, was ornamented with grotesque figures; while the walls were also partially formed of squat, semi-human statues, set upon huge, triangular shafts. In the spaces between these outlandish pilasters there had once been some sort of decorations. A great many photos were taken here.

As for the floor, it was divided in all directions by low walls. About five and a half feet in height, these walls separated the great room into perhaps a hundred triangular compartments, each about the size of an ordinary living room. Broad openings, about five feet square, provided free access from one compartment to any other. The men from the earth, by standing on tiptoes, could see over and beyond this system.

"Wonder if these walls were supposed to cut off the view?" speculated the doctor. "I mean, do you suppose that the Mercurians were such short people as that?" His question had to go unanswered.

They stepped into the nearest compartment, and were on the point of pronouncing it bare, when Jackson, with an exclamation, excitedly brushed away some of the dust and showed that the presumably solid walls were really chests of

25

drawers. Shallow things of that peculiar metal, these drawers numbered several hundred to the compartment. In the whole building there must have been millions.

Once more the dust was carefully removed, revealing a layer of those curious rolls or reels, exactly similar to what had been found in the tool chest in the shell works. A careful examination of the metallic tape showed nothing whatever to the naked eye, although the doctor fancied that he made out some strange characters on the little boxes themselves.

His view was shortly proved. Finding drawer after drawer to contain a similar display, varying from one to a dozen of the diminutive ribbons, Van Emmon adopted the plan of gently blowing away the dust from the faces of the drawers before opening them. This revealed the fact that each of the shallow things was neatly labeled!

Instantly the three were intent upon this fresh clue. The markings were very faint and delicate, the slightest touch being enough to destroy them. To the untrained eye, they resembled ancient Egyptian hieroglyphics; to the archeologist, they meant that a brand-new system of ideographs had been found.

Suddenly Jackson straightened up and looked about with a new interest. He went to one of the square doorways and very carefully removed the dust from a small plate on the lintel. He need not have been so careful; engraved in the solid metal was a single character, plainly in the same language as the other ideographs.

The architect smiled triumphantly into the inquiring eyes of his friends. "I won't have to eat my hat," said he. "This is a sure-enough city, all right, and this is its library!"

Smith was still busy on the little machine when they returned to the cube. He said that one part of it had disappeared, and was busily engaged in filing a bit of steel to take its place. As soon as it was ready, he thought, they could see what the apparatus meant.

The three had brought a large number of the reels. They were confident that a microscopic search of the ribbons would disclose something to bear out Jackson's theory that the great structure was really a repository for books, or whatever corresponded with books on Mercury.

"But the main thing," said the doctor, enthusiastically, "is to get over to the 'twilight band.' I'm beginning to have all sorts of wild hopes."

Jackson urged that they first visit the big "mansion" on the outskirts of this place; he said he felt sure, somehow, that it would be worth while. But Van Emmon backed up the doctor, and the architect had to be content with an agreement to return in case their trip was futile.

Inside of a few minutes the cube was being drawn steadily over toward the left or western edge of the planet's sunlit face. As it moved, all except Smith kept close watch on the ground below. They made out town after town, as well as separate buildings; and on the roads were to be seen a great many of those octagonal structures, all motionless.

After several hundred miles of this, the surface abruptly sloped toward what had clearly been the bed of an ocean. No sign of habitations here, however; so apparently the water had disappeared *after* the humans had gone.

This ancient sea ended a short distance from the district they were seeking. A little more travel brought them to a point where the sun cast as much shadow as light on the surface. It was here they descended, coming to rest on a sunlit knoll which overlooked a small, building-filled valley.

According to Kinney's apparatus, there was about one-fortieth the amount of air that exists on the earth. Of water vapor there was a trace; but all their search revealed no human life. Not only that, but there was no trace of lower animals; there was not even a lizard, much less a bird. And even the most ancient-looking of the sculptures showed no creatures of the air; only huge, antediluvian monsters were ever depicted.

They took a great many photos as a matter of course. Also, they investigated some of the big, octagonal machines in the streets, finding them to be similar to the great "tanks" that were used in the war, except that they did not have the characteristic caterpillar tread; their eight faces were so

27

linked together that the entire affair could roll, after a jolting, slab-sided, flopping fashion. Inside were curious engines, and sturdy machines designed to throw the cannon-shells they had seen; no explosive was employed, apparently, but centrifugal force generated in whirling wheels. Apparently these cars, or chariots, were universally used.

The explorers returned to the cube, where they found that Smith, happening to look out a window, had spied a pond not far off. The three visited it and found, on its banks, the first green stuff they had seen; a tiny, flowerless salt grass, very scarce. It bordered a slimy, bluish pool of absolutely still fluid. Nobody would call it water. They took a few samples of it and went back.

And within a few minutes the doctor slid a small glass slide into his microscope, and examined the object with much satisfaction. What he saw was a tiny, gelatinlike globule; among scientists it is known as the *amoeba*. It is the simplest known form of life—the so-called "single cell." It had been the first thing to live on that planet, and apparently it was also the last.

V

THE CLOSED DOOR

As THEY NEARED Jackson's pet "mansion" each man paid close attention to the intervening blocks. For the most part these were simply shapeless ruins; heaps of what had once been, perhaps, brick or stone. Once they allowed the cube to rest on the top of one of these mounds; but the sky-car's great weight merely sank it into the mass. There was nothing under it save that same sandy dust.

Apparently the locality they were approaching had been set aside as a very exclusive residence district for the élite of the country. Possibly it contained the homes of the royalty, assuming that there had been a royalty. At any rate the

conspicuous structure Jackson had selected was certainly the
home of the most important member of that colony.

When the three, once more in their helmets and suits,
stood before the low, broad portico which protected the entrance to that edifice, the first thing they made out was an
ornamental frieze running across the face. In the same bold,
realistic style as the other sculpture, there was depicted a
hand-to-hand battle between two groups of those half savage,
half cultured monstrosities. And in the background was
shown a glowing orb, obviously the sun.

"See that?" exclaimed the doctor. "The size of that sun,
I mean! Compare it with the way old Sol looks now!"

They took a single glance at the great ball of fire over
their heads; nine times the size it always seemed at home, it
contrasted sharply with the rather small ball shown in the
carvings.

"Understand?" the doctor went on. "When that sculpture
was made, Mercury was little nearer the sun than the earth
is now!"

The builder was hugely impressed. He asked, eagerly:
"Then probably the people became as highly developed as
we?"

Van Emmon nodded approvingly, but the doctor opposed.
"No; I think not, Jackson. Mercury never did have as much
air as the earth, and consequently had much less oxygen.
And the struggle for existence," he went on, watching to see
if the geologist approved each point as he made it, "the
struggle for life is, in the last analysis, a struggle for oxygen.

"So I would say that life was a pretty strenuous propos-
ition here, while it lasted. Perhaps they were—" He stopped,
then added: "What I can't understand is, how did it happen
that their affairs came to such an abrupt end? And why don't
we see any—er—indications?"

"Skeletons?" The architect shuddered. Next second, though,
his face lit up with a thought. "I remember reading that
electricity will decompose bone, in time. And then he shuddered again as his foot stirred that lifeless, impalpable dust.
Was it possible?

THE LORD OF DEATH

As they passed into the great house the first thing they noted was the floor, undivided, dust-covered, and bare, except for what had perhaps been rugs. The shape was the inevitable equilateral triangle; and here, with a certain magnificent disregard for precedent, the builders had done away with a ceiling entirely, and instead had sloped the three walls up till they met in a single point, a hundred feet overhead. The effect was massively simple.

In one corner a section of the floor was elevated perhaps three feet above the rest, and directly back of this was a broad doorway, set in a short wall. The three advanced at once toward it.

Here the electric torch came in very handy. It disclosed a poorly lighted stairway, very broad, unrailed, and preposterously steep. The steps were each over three feet high.

"Difference in gravitation," said the doctor, in response to Jackson's questioning look. "Easy enough for the old-timers, perhaps." They struggled up the flight as best they could, reaching the top after over five minutes of climbing.

Perhaps it was the reaction from this exertion; at all events each felt a distinct loss of confidence as, after regaining their wind, they again began to explore. Neither said anything about it to the others; but each noted a queer sense of foreboding, far more disquieting than either of them had felt when investigating anything else. It may have been due to the fact that, in their hurry, they had not stopped to eat.

The floor they were on was fairly well lighted with the usual oval windows. The space was open, except that it contained the same kind of dividing walls they had found in the library. Here, however, each compartment contained but one opening, and that not uniformly placed. In fact, as the three noted with a growing uneasiness, it was necessary to pass through every one of them in order to reach the corner farthest from the ladderlike stairs. Why it should make them uneasy, neither could have said.

When they were almost through the labyrinth, Van Emmon, after standing on tiptoes for the tenth time, in order to locate himself, noted something that had escaped their attention before. "These compartments used to be covered over," he said, for some reason lowering his voice. He pointed out niches in the walls, such as undoubtedly once held the ends of heavy timbers. "What was this place, anyhow? A trap?"

Unconsciously they lightened their steps as they neared the last compartment. They found, as expected, that it was another stairwell. Van Emmon turned the light upon every corner of the place before going any further; but except for a formless heap of rubbish in one corner, which they did not investigate, the place was as bare as the rest of the floor.

Again they climbed, this time for a much shorter distance; but Jackson, slightly built chap that he was, needed a little help on the steep stairs. They were not sorry that they had reached the uppermost floor of the mansion. It was somewhat better lighted than the floor below, and they were relieved to find that the triangular compartments did not have the significant niches in their walls. Their spirits rose perceptibly.

At the corner farthest from the stairs one of the walls rose straight to the ceiling, completely cutting off a rather large triangle. The three paid no attention to the other compartments, but went straight to what they felt sure was the most vital spot in the place. And their feelings were justified with a vengeance when they saw that the usual doorway in this wall was protected by something that had, so far, been entirely missing everywhere else.

It was barred by a heavy door.

For several minutes the doctor, the geologist, and the architect stood before it. Neither would have liked to admit that he would just as soon leave that door unopened. All the former uneasiness came back. It was all the more inexplicable, with the brilliant sunlight only a few feet away, that each should have felt chilled by the place.

"Wonder if it's locked?" remarked Van Emmon. He pressed against the dust-covered barrier, half expecting it to turn to dust; but evidently it had been made of the time-defying alloy. It stood firm. And to all appearances it was nearly air-tight.

"Well!" said the doctor suddenly, so that the other two

started nervously. "The door's got to come down; that's all!"
They looked around; there was no furniture, no loose piece
of material of any kind. Van Emmon straightway backed
away from the door about six feet, and the others followed
his example.

"All together!" grunted the geologist; and the three aluminum-armored monsters charged the door. It shook under the
impact; a shower of dust fell down; and they saw that they
had loosened the thing.

"Once more!" This time a wide crack showed all around the
edge of the door, and the third attempt finished the job.
Noiselessly—for their was no air to carry the sound—but with
a heavy jar which all three felt through their feet, the barrier
went flat on the floor beyond.

At the same instant a curious, invisible wave, like a tiny
puff of wind, floated out of the darkness and passed by the
three men from the earth. Each noticed it, but neither men-
tioned it at the time. Van Emmon was already searching the
darkness with the torch.

Apparently it was only an anteroom. A few feet beyond
was another wall, and in it stood another door, larger and
heavier than the first. The three did not stop; they immediately tried their strength on this one also.

After a half dozen attempts without so much as shaking
the massive affair—"It's no use," panted the geologist, wish-
ing that he could get a handkerchief to his forehead. "We
can't loosen it without tools."

Jackson was for trying again, but the doctor agreed with
Van Emmon. They reflected that they had been away from
Smith long enough, anyhow. The cube was out of sight from
where they were.

Van Emmon turned the light on the walls of the anteroom,
and found, on a shelf at one end, a neat pile of those little
reels, eleven in all. He pocketed the lot. There was nothing
else.

Jackson and Kinney started to go. They retreated as far
into the main room as their telephone wires would allow.
Still the geologist held back.

THE LORD OF DEATH

"Come on," said the doctor uneasily. "It's getting cold."

Next second they stopped short, nerves on edge, at a strange exclamation from Van Emmon. They looked around to see him pointing his light directly at the floor. Even in that unnatural suit of mail, his attitude was one of horror.

"Look here," he said in a low, strained voice. They went to his side, and instinctively glanced behind them before looking at what lay in the dust.

It was the imprint of an enormous human foot.

The first thing that greeted the ears of the explorers upon taking off their suits in the sky-car, was the exultant voice of Smith. He was too excited to notice anything out of the way in their manner; he was almost dancing in front of his bench, where the unknown machine, now reconstructed, stood belted to a small electric-motor.

"It runs!" he was shouting. "You got here just in time!" He began to fumble with a switch.

"What of it?" remarked the doctor in the bland tone which he kept for occasions when Smith needed calming. "What will it do if it does run?"

The engineer looked blank. "Why—" Then he remembered, and picked up one of the reels at random. "There's a clamp here just the right size to hold one of these," he explained, fitting the ribbon into place and threading its free end into a loop on a spool which looked as though made for it. But his excitement had passed; he now cautiously set a small anvil between himself and the apparatus, and then, with the aid of a long stick, he threw on the current.

For a moment nothing happened, save the hum of the motor. Then a strange, leafy rustling sounded from the mechanism, and next, without any warning, a high-pitched voice, nasal and plaintive but distinctly human, spoke from the big metal disk.

The words were unintelligible. The language was totally unlike anything ever heard on the earth. And yet, deliberately if somewhat cringingly, the voice proceeded with what was apparently a recitation. There were modulations, pauses, sentences; but seemingly the paragraphs were all short and to the point.

As the thing went on the four men came closer and watched the operation of the machine. The ribbon unrolled slowly; it was plain that, if the one topic occupied the whole reel, then it must have the length of an ordinary chapter. And as the voice continued, certain dramatic qualities came out and governed the words, utterly incomprehensible though they were. There was a real thrill to it.

After a while they stopped the thing. "No use listening to this now," as the doctor said. "We've got to learn a good deal more about these people before we can guess what it all means."

And yet, although all were very hungry, on Jackson's suggestion they tried out one of the "records" that was brought from that baffling anteroom. Smith was very much interested in that unopened door, and Van Emmon was in the midst of it when Jackson started the motor.

The geologist's words stuck in his throat. The disk was actually shaking with the vibrations of a most terrific voice. Prodigiously loud and powerful, its booming, resonant bass smote the ears like the roll of thunder. It was irresistible in its force, compelling in its assurance, masterful and strong to an overpowering degree. Involuntarily the men from the earth stepped back.

On it roared and rumbled, speaking the same language as that of the other record; but whereas the first speaker merely *used* the words, the last speaker demolished them. One felt that he had extracted every ounce of power in the language, leaving it weak and flabby, unfit for further use. He threw out his sentences as though done with them; not boldly, not defiantly, least of all, tentatively, he spoke with a certainty and force that came from a knowledge that he could compel, rather than induce his hearers to believe.

It took a little nerve to shut him off; Van Emmon was the one who did it. Somehow they all felt immensely relieved

34

when the gigantic voice was silenced; and at once began discussing the thing with great earnestness. Jackson was for assuming that the first record was worn and old, the last one, fresh and new; but after examining both tapes under a glass, and seeing how equally clear cut and sharp the impressions all were, they agreed that the extraordinary voice they had heard was practically true to life.

They tried out the rest of the records in that batch, finding that they were all by the same speaker. Nowhere among the ribbons brought from the library was another of his making, although a great number of different voices was included; neither was there another talker with a fifth the volume, the resonance, the absolute power of conviction that this unknown colossus possessed.

Of course this is no place to describe the laborious process of interpreting these documents, records of a past which was gone before earth's mankind had even begun. The work involved the study of countless photos, covering everything from inscriptions to parts of machinery, and other details which furnished clue after clue to that superancient language. It was not deciphered, in fact, until several years after the explorers had submitted their finds to the world's foremost lexicographers, antiquarians and paleontologists. Even today some of it is disputed.

But right here is, most emphatically, the place to insert the tale told by that unparalleled voice. And incredible though it may seem, as judged by the standards of the peoples of this earth, the account is fairly proved by the facts uncovered by the expedition. It would be but begging the question to doubt the genuineness of the thing; and if, understanding the language, one were to hear the original as it fell, word for word from the iron mouth of Strokor° the Great—hearing, one would believe; none could doubt, nor would.

And so it does not do him justice to set it down in ordinary print. One must imagine the story being related by

---

°Translator's note—In the Mercurian language, stroke means iron, or heart.

Stentor himself; must conceive of each word falling like the blow of a mammoth sledge. The tale was not told—it was *bellowed;* and this is how it ran:

PART II

THE STORY

I

THE MAN

I AM STROKOR, son of Strok, the armorer. I am Strokor, a maker of tools of war; Strokor, the mightiest man in the world; Strokor, whose wisdom outwitted the hordes of Klow; Strokor, who has never feared, and never failed. Let him who dares, dispute it. I—I am Strokor!

In my youth I was, as now, the marvel of all who saw. I was ever robust and daring, and naught but much older, bigger lads could outdo me. I balked at nothing, be it a game or a battle; it was, and forever shall be, my chief delight to best all others.

'Twas from my mother that I gained my huge frame and sound heart. In truth, I am very like her, now that I think upon it. She, too, was indomitable in battle, and famed for her liking for strife. No doubt 'twas her stalwart figure that caught my father's fancy.

Aye, my mother was a very likely woman, but she boasted no brains. "I need no cunning," I remember she said; and he who was so unlucky in battle as to fall into her hands could vouch for the truth of it—as long as he lived, which would not be long. She was a grand woman, slow to anger and a match for many a good pair of men. Often, as a lad, have I carried the marks of her punishment for the most of a year.

And thus it seems that I owe my head to my father. He was a marvelously clever man, dexterous with hand and brain alike. Moreover, he was no weakling; perchance I should credit him with some of my agility, for he was famed as a gymnast, though not a powerful one. 'Twas he who taught me how to disable my enemy with a mere clutch of the neck at a certain spot.

But Strok, the armorer, was feared most because of his brain, and his knack of using his mind to the undoing of others. And he taught me all that he knew; taught me all that he had learned in a lifetime of fighting for the emperor, of mending the complicated machines in the armory, of contact with the chemists who wrought the secret alloy, and the chiefs who led the army.

Some of this he taught me when I was not yet a man. Why he should have done so, I know not, save that he seemed to value my affection, and liked not my mother's demands that I heed her call, not his. At all events, I oft found his shop a place of refuge from her wrath; and I early came to value his teachings.

When I became a man he abruptly ended the practice. I think he saw that I was become as dexterous as he with the tools of the craft, and he feared lest I know more then he. Well he might; the day I realized this I laughed long and loud. And from that time forth he taught me, not because he chose to, but because I bent a chisel in my bare hands, before his eyes, and told him his place.

Many times he strove to trick me, and more than once he all but caught me in some trap. He was a crafty man, and relied not upon brawn, but upon wits. Yet I was ever on the watch, and I but learned the more from him.

"Ye are very kind," I mocked him one morning. When I had taken my seat a huge weight had dropped from above and crushed my stool to splinters, much as it would have crushed my skull had I not leaped instantly aside. "Ye are kinder than most fathers, who teach their sons nothing at all."

He foamed at his mouth in his rage and discomfiture. "Insolent whelp!" he snarled. "Thou art quick as a cat on thy feet!"

But I was not to be appeased by words. I smote him on the chest with my bare hand, so that he fell on the far side of the room. "Let that be a warning," I told him, when he had recovered, some time later. "If ye have any more tricks, try them for, not on, me." Which I claim to be a neat twist of words.

It was not long after that when I saw a change in my father. He no longer tried to snare me; instead, he began, of his own free will, to train my mind to other than warlike things. At first, I was suspicious enough. I looked for new traps, and watched all the closer. I told him that his next try would surely be his last, and I meant it.

But the time came when I saw that my father was reconciled to his master. I saw that he genuinely admitted my prowess; and where he formerly envied me, he now took great pride in all I accomplished, and claimed that it was but his own brains acting through my body.

I let him indulge in the conceit. I grudged it not to him, so long as he taught me. In truth, he was so eager to add to my store of facts, so intent upon filling my head with what filled his, that at times I was fairly compelled to stop him, lest I tire.

My mother opposed all this. "The lad needs none of thy wiles," she gibed. "He is no stripling; he is a man's man, and a fit son of his mother."

"Aye," quoth my father slyly. "He has thy muscle and thy courage. Thank Jon, he hath not thy empty head!"

Whereat she flew at him. Had she caught him, she would have destroyed him, such was her rage; and afterwards she would have mourned her folly and mayhap have injured herself; for she loved him greatly. But he stepped aside just in the nick of time, and she crashed into the wall behind him with such force that she was senseless for a time. I remember it well.

And yet, to give credit where credit is due, I must admit that I owe a great deal to that gray-beard, Maka, the stargazer. But for him, perchance, the name of Strokor would mean but little, for 'twas he who gave me ambition.

Truly it was an uncommon affair, my first meeting with him. Now that I shake my memory for it, it seems that something else of like consequence came to pass on the same occasion. Curious; but I have not thought on it for many days.

Yes, it is true; I met Maka on the very morn that I first laid eyes on the girl Ave.

I was returning from the northland at the time. A rumor had come down to Vlama that one of the people in the snow country had seen a lone specimen of the mulikka. Now these were but a myth. No man living remembers when the carvings on the House of Learning were made, and all the wise men say that it hath been ages since any being other than man roamed the world. Yet, I was young. I determined to search for the thing anyhow; and 'twas only after wasting many days in the snow that I cursed my luck, and turned back.

I was afoot, for the going was too rough for my chariot. I had not yet quit the wilderness before, from a height, I spied a group of people ascending from the valley. Knowing not whether they be friends or foes, I hid beside the path up which they must come; for I was weary and wanting no strife.

Yet I became alert enough when the three—they were two ditch-tenders, one old, one young, and a girl—came within earshot. For they were quarreling. It seemed that the young man, who was plainly eager to gain the girl, had fouled in a try to force her favor. The older man chided him hotly.

And just when they came opposite my rock, the younger man, whose passion had got the better of him, suddenly tripped the older, so that he fell upon the ledge and would have fallen to his death on the rocks below had not the girl, crying out in her terror, leaped forward and caught his hand.

At once the ditch-tender took the lass about the waist, and strove to pull her away. For a moment she held fast, and in that moment I, Strokor, stood forth from behind the rock.

Now, be it known that I am no champion of weaklings. I have no liking for the troubles of others; enough of my own, say I. I was but angered that the ditch-tender should have

39

done the trick so clumsily, and upon an old man, at that. I cared not for the gray beard, nor what became of the chit. I clapped the trickster upon the shoulder and spun him about.

"Ye clumsy coward!" I jeered. "Have ye had no practice that ye should trip the old one no better than that?"

"Who are ye?" he stuttered, like the coward he was. I laughed and helped the chit drag Maka—for it was he—up to safety.

"I am a far better man than ye," I said, not caring to give my name. "And I can show ye how the thing should be done. Come; at me, if ye are a man!"

At that he dashed upon me; and such was his fear of ridicule—for the girl was laughing him to scorn now—he put up a fair, stiff fight. But I forgot my weariness when he foully clotted me on the head with a stone. I drove at him with all the speed and suddenness my father had taught me, caught the fellow by the ankle, and brought him down atop me.

The rest was easy. I bent my knee under his middle, and tossed him high. In a flash I was upon my feet, and caught him from behind. And in another second I had rushed him to the cliff; and when he turned to save himself, I tripped him as neatly as father himself could have done it, so that the fellow will guard the ditch no more, save in the caverns of Hofe.

I laughed and picked up my pack. My head hurt a bit from the fellow's blow, but a little water would do for that. I started to go.

"Ye are a brave man!" cried the girl. I turned carelessly, and then, quite for the first time, I had a real look at her.

She was in no way like any woman I had seen. All of them had been much like the men: brawny and close-knit, as well fitted for their work as are men for war. But this chit was all but slender; not skinny, but prettily rounded out, and soft like. I cannot say that I admired her at first glance; she seemed fit only to look at, not to live. I was minded of some of the ancient carvings, which show delicate, lightly built animals that have long since been killed off; graceful trifles that rested the eye.

As for the old man: "Aye, thou art brave, and wondrous strong, my lad," said he, still a bit shaky from his close call. I was pleased with the acknowledgment, and turned back.

"It was nothing," I told them; and I recounted some of my exploits, notably one in which I routed a raiding party of men from Klow, six in all, carrying in two alive on my shoulders. "I am the son of Strok, the armorer."

"Ye are Strokor!" marveled the girl, staring at me as though I were a god. Then she threw back her head and stepped close.

"I am Ave. This is Maka; he is my uncle, but best known as a star-gazer. My father was Durok, the engine-maker." She watched my face.

"Durok?" I knew him well. My father had said that he was quite as brainy as himself. "He were a fine man, Ave."

"Aye," said she proudly. She stepped closer; I could not but see how like him she was, though a woman. And next second she laid a hand on my arm.

"I am yet a free woman, Strokor. Hast thou picked thy mate?" And her cheeks flamed.

Now, 'twas not my first experience of the kind. Many women had looked like that at me before. But I had always been a man's man, and had ever heeded my father's warning to have naught whatever to do with women. "They are the worst trick of all," he told me; and I had never forgot. Belike I owe much of my power to just this.

But Ave had acted too quickly for me to get away. I laughed again, and shook her off.

"I will have naught to do with ye," I told her, civilly enough. "When I am ready to take a woman, I shall take her; not before."

At that the blood left her face; she stood very straight, and her eyes flashed dangerously. Were she a man I should have stood on my guard. But she made no move; only the softness in her eyes gave way to such a savage look that I was filled with amaze.

41

And thus I left them; the old man calling down the blessing of Jon upon me for having saved his life, and the chit glaring after me as though no curses would suffice.

A right queer matter, I thought at the time. I guessed not what would come of it; not then.

II

THE VISION

'TWAS A FORTNIGHT later, more or less, when next I saw Maka. I was lumbering along in my chariot, feeling most uncomfortable under the eyes of my friends; for one foot of my machine had a loose link, and 'twas flapping absurdly. And I liked it none too well when Maka stopped his own rattletrap in front of mine, and came running to my window. Next moment I forgot his impertinence.

"Strokor," he whispered, his face alive with excitement, "thou art a brave lad, and didst save my life. Now, know you that a party of the men of Klow have secreted themselves under the stairway behind the emperor's throne. They have killed the guards, and will of a certainty kill the emperor, too!"

" 'Twould serve the dolt right," I replied, for I really cared but little. "But why have ye come to me, old man? I am but a lieutenant in the armory; I am not the captain of the palace guard."

"Because," he answered, gazing at me very pleasingly, "thou couldst dispose of the whole party single handed—there are but four—and gain much glory for thyself."

"By Jon!" I swore, vastly delighted; and without stopping to ask Maka whence he had got his knowledge, I went at once to the spot. However, when I got back, I sought the star-gazer—I ought to mention that I had no trouble with the louts, and that the emperor himself saw me finishing off

42

the last of them—I sought the star-gazer and demanded how he had known.

"Hast ever heard of Edam?" he inquired in return.

"Edam?" I had not; the name was strange to me. "Who is he?"

"A man as young as thyself, but a mere stripling," quoth Maka. "He was a pupil of mine when I taught in the House of Learning. Of late he has turned to prophecy; and it is fair remarkable how well the lad doth guess. At all events, 'twas he, Strokor, who told me of the plot. He saw it in a dream."

"Then Edam must yet be in Vlama," said I, "if he were able to tell ye. Canst bring him to me? I would know him."

And so it came about that, on the eve of that same day, Maka brought Edam to my house. I remember it well; for 'twas the same day that the emperor, in gratitude of my little service in the anteroom, had relieved me from my post in the armory and made me captain of the palace guard. I was thus become the youngest captain, also the biggest and strongest; and, as will soon appear, by far the longest-headed.

I was in high good humor, and had decided to celebrate with a feast. So when my two callers arrived, I sat them down before a meal such as cost a tenth* of my year's salary.

I served not only the usual products of the field, variously prepared, but as a special gift from the emperor's own stock, a piece of mulikka meat, frozen, which had been found in the northland by some geologists a few years aback. It had been kept in the palace icing-room all this time, and was in prime condition. Maka and I enjoyed it overmuch, but Edam would touch it not.

He was a slightly built lad, not at all the sturdy man that I am, but of less than half the weight. His head, too, was

---

*Since Mercury had no moon, its people never coined a word to correspond with our "month," and for the same reason they never had a week. Their time was reckoned only in days, years, and fractions of the two.

unlike mine; his forehead was wide as well as tall, and his eyes were mild as a slave's.

"Ye are very young to be a prophet," I said to him, after we were filled, and the slaves had cleared away our litter. "Tell me: hast foretold anything else that has come to pass?"

"Aye," he replied, not at all boldly, but what some call modestly. "I prophesied the armistice which now stands between our empire and Klow's."

"Is this true?" I demanded of Maka. The old man bowed his head gravely and looked upon the young man with far more respect than I felt. He added:

"Tell Strokor the dream thou hadst two nights ago, Edam. It were a right strange thing, whether true or no."

The stripling shifted his weight on his stool, and moved the bowl closer. Then he thrust his pipe deep into it, and let the liquid flow slowly out his nostrils.*

"I saw this," he began, "immediately before rising, and after a very light supper; so I know that it was a vision from Jon, and not of my own making.

"I was standing upon the summit of a mountain, and gazing down upon a very large, fertile valley. It was heavily wooded, dark green and inviting. But what first drew my attention was a great number of animals moving about *in the air*. They were passing strange affairs, some large, some small, variously colored, and all covered with the same sort of fur, quite unlike any hair I have ever seen."

"In the air?" I echoed, recovering from my astonishment. Then I laughed mightily. "Man, ye must be crazy! There is no animal can live in the air! Ye must mean in the water or on land."

"Nay," interposed the star-gazer. "Thou hast never studied the stars, Strokor, or thou wouldst know that there be a num-

---

*A curious custom among the Mercurians, who had no tobacco. There is no other way to explain some of the carvings. Doubtless the liquid was sweet-smelling, and perhaps slightly narcotic.

ber of them which, through the enlarging tube, show themselves to be round worlds, like unto our own.

"And it doth further appear that these other worlds also have air like this we breathe, and that some have less, while others have even more. From what Edam has told me," finished the old man, "I judge that his vision took place on Jeos,† a world much larger than ours according to my calculations, and doubtless having enough air to permit very light creatures to move about in it."

"Go on," said I to Edam, good-humoredly. "I be ever willing to believe anything strange when my stomach is full."

The dreamer had taken no offense. "Then I bent my gaze closer, as I am always able, in visions. And I saw that the greenery was most remarkably dense, tangled and luxuriant to a degree not ever seen here. And moving about in it was the most extraordinary collection of beings that I have ever laid these eyes upon.

"There were some huge creatures, quite as tall as thy house, Strokor, with legs as big around as that huge chest of thine. They had tails, as had our ancient mulikka, save that these were terrific things, as long and as big as the trunk of a large tree. I know not their names.‡

"And then, at the other extreme, was a tiny creature of the air, which moved with a musical hum. It could have hid under thy finger-nail, Strokor, yet it had a tiny sharp-pointed bill, with which it stung most aggravatingly. And between these two there were any number of creatures of varying size and shape.

"But nowhere was there a sign of a man. True, there was one hairy, grotesque creature which hung by its hands and feet from the tree-tops, very like thee in some way, Strokor; but its face and head were those of a brainless beast, not of a man. Nowhere was a creature like me or thee.

"And the most curious thing was this: Although there were ten times as many of these creatures, big and little, to the

---

†The Mercurian word for earth.
‡Probably the dinosaur.

same space as on our world, yet there was no great amount of strife. In truth, there is far more combat and destruction among we men than among the beasts.

"And," he spoke most earnestly, as though he would not care to be disbelieved, "I saw fathers fight to protect their young!"

I near fell from my stool in my amaze. Never in all my life had I heard a thing so far from the fact. "What!" I shouted. "Ye sit there like a sane man, and tell me ye saw fathers fight for their young?"

He nodded his head, still very gravely. I fell silent for want of words,.but Maka put in a thought. "It would appear, Strokor, that it be not so much of an effort for beings to live, there on Jeos, as here. Perchance 'tis the greater amount of vegetation; at all accounts, the animals need not prey upon one another so generally; and that, then, would explain why some have energy enough to waste in the care of their young."

"I can understand," I said, very slowly. "I can understand why a mother will fight for her babes; 'tis reasonable enough, no doubt. But as for fathers doing the same—Edam, dost mean to say that *all* creatures on Jeos do this?"

"Nay; only some. It may be that fewer than half of the varieties have the custom. Howbeit, 'tis a beautiful one. When the vision ended I was right loath to go."

"Faugh!" I spat upon the ground. "Such softness makes me ill! I be glad I were born in a man's world, where I can take a man's chances. I want no favoring. If I am strong enough to live, I live; if not, I die. What more can I ask?"

"Aye, my lad!" said Maka approvingly. "This be a world for the strong. There is no room here for others; there is scarce enough food for those who, thanks to their strength, do survive." He slipped the gold band from off his wrist, and held it up for Jon to see. "Here, Strokor, a pledge! A pledge to—the survival of the fittest!"

"A neat, neat wording!" I roared, as I took the pledge with him. Then we both stopped short. Edam had not joined us.

"Edam, my lad," spake the old man, "ye will take the pledge with us?"

THE LORD OF DEATH

The stripling's eyes were troubled. Well he knew that, once he refused such an act, he were no longer welcome in my house, nor in Maka's. But when he looked around it were bravely enough.

"Men, I have neither the strength of the one nor the brains of the other of ye. I am but a watchmaker; I live because of my skill with the little wheels.

"I have no quarrel with either of ye." He got to his feet, and started to the door. "But I cannot take the pledge with ye.

"I have seen a wondrous thing, and I love it. And, though I know not why—I feel that Jon has willed it for Jeos to see a new race of men, a race even better than ours."

I leaped to my feet. "Better than ours! Mean ye to say, stripling, that there can be a better man than Strokor?"

I full expected him to shrink from me in fear; I was able to crush him with one blow. But he stood his ground; nay, stepped forward and laid a hand easily upon my shoulder.

"Strokor—ye are more than a man; ye are two men in one. There is no finer—I say it fair. And yet, I doubt not that there can be, and will be, a better!"

And with that such a curious expression came into his face, such a glow of some strange kind of warmth, that I let my hand drop and suffered him to depart in peace—such was my wonder.

Besides, any miserable lout could have destroyed the lad.

Maka sat deep in thought for a time, and when he did speak he made no mention of the lad who had just quit us. Instead, he looked me over, long and earnestly, and at the end he shook his head sorrowfully and sighed:

"Thou art the sort of a son I would have had, Strokor, given the wits of thy father to hold a woman like thy mother. And thou didst save my life."

He mused a little longer, then roused himself and spake sharply: "Thou art a vain man, Strokor!"

"Aye," I agreed, willingly enough. "And none has better cause than I!"

He would not acknowledge the quip. "Thou hast every-

47

thing needful to tickle thy vanity. Thou hast the envy of those who note thy strength, the praise of them who love thy courage, and the respect of they who value thy brains. All these thou hast—and yet ye have not that which is best!"

I thought swiftly and turned on him with a frown: "Mean ye that I am not handsome enough?"

"Nay, Strokor," quoth the star-gazer. "There be none handsomer in this world, no matter what the standard of any other, such as Edam's Jeos.

"It is not that. It is, that thou hast no ambition."

I considered this deeply. At first thought it was not true; had I not always made it a point to best my opponent? From my youth it had been ever my custom to succeed where bigger bodies and older minds had failed. Was not this ambition?

But before I disputed the point with Maka, I saw what he meant. I had no *final* ambition, no ultimate goal for which to strive. I had been content from year to year to outdo each rival as he came before me; and now, with mind and body alike in the pink of condition, I was come to the place where none durst stand before me.

"Ye are right, Maka," I admitted, not because I cared to gratify his conceit, but because it were always for my own good to own up when wrong, that I might learn the better. "Ye are right; I need to decide upon a life-purpose. What have ye thought?"

The old man was greatly pleased. "Our talk with Edam brought it all before me. Know you, Strokor, that the survival of the fittest is a rule which governs man as well as men. It applies to the entire population, Strokor, just as truly as to me or thee.

"In fine, we men who are now the sole inhabitants of this world, are descended from a race of people who survived solely because they were fitter than the mulikka, fitter than the reptiles, the fittest, by far, of all the creatures.

"That being the case, it is plain that in time either our empire, or that of Klow's, must triumph over the other. And that which remains shall be the fittest!"

48

THE LORD OF DEATH

"Hold!" I cried. "Why cannot matters remain just as they now are—and forever?"

"That," he said rapidly, "is because thou knowest so little about the future of this world. But I am famed as a student of the heavens; and I tell thee it is possible, by means of certain delicate measuring instruments, together with the highest mathematics, to keep a very close watch upon the course of our world. And we now know that our year is much shorter than it was in the days of the mulikka."

I nodded my head. "Rightly enough, since our days are become steadily longer, for some mysterious reason."

"A reason no longer a mystery," quoth Maka. "It is now known that the sun is a very powerful magnet, and that it is constantly pulling upon our world and bringing it nearer and nearer to himself. That is why it hath become slightly warmer during the past hundred years; the records show it plain. And the same influence has caused the lengthening of our day."

He stopped and let me think. Soon I saw it clearly enough; a time must come when the increasing warmth of the sun would stifle all forms of vegetable life, and that would mean the choking of mankind. It might take untold centuries; yet, plainly enough, the world must some day become too small for even those who now remained upon it.

Suddenly I leaped to my feet and strode the room in my excitement. "Ye are right, Maka!" I shouted, thoroughly aroused. "There cannot always be the two empires. In time one or the other must prevail; Jon has willed it. And"—I stopped short and stared at him—"I need not tell ye which it shall be!"

"I knew thou wouldst see the light, Strokor! Thou hast thy father's brains."

I sat me down, but instantly leaped up again, such was my enthusiasm. "Maka," I cried, "our emperor is not the man for the place! It is true that he were a brave warrior in his youth; he won the throne fairly. And we have suffered him to keep it because he is a wise man, and because we have had little trouble with the men of Klow since their defeat two generations agone.

"But he, today, is content to sit at his ease and quote platitudes about 'live and let live.' Faugh! I am ashamed that I should even have given ear to him!"

I stopped short and glared at the old man. "Maka—hark ye well! If it be the will of Jon to decide between the men of Klow and the men of Vlamaland, then it is my intent to take a hand in this decision!"

"Aye, my lad," he said tranquilly; and then added, quite as though he knew what my answer must be: "How do ye intend to go about it?"

"Like a man! I, Strokor, shall become the emperor!"

III

THE THRONE

A SMALL STORM had come up while Maka and I were talking. Now, as he was about to quit me, the clouds were clearing away and an occasional stroke of lightning came down. One of these, however, hit the ground such a short distance away that both of us could smell the smoke.

My mind was more alive than it had ever been before. "Now, what caused that, Maka? The lightning, I mean; we have it nearly every day, yet I have never thought to question it before."

"It is no mystery, my lad," quoth Maka, dodging into his chariot, so that he was not wet. "I myself have watched the thing from the top of high mountains, where the air is so light that a man can scarce get enough to fill his lungs; and I say unto you that, were it not for what air we have, we should have naught save the lightning. The space about the air is full of it."

He started his engine, then leaned out into the rain and said softly: "Hold fast to what thy father has taught thee, Strokor. Have nothing to do with the women. 'Tis a man's job ahead of thee, and the future of the empire is in thy hands.

"And," as he clattered off, "fill not thy head with wonderings about the lightning."

"Aye," said I right earnestly, and immediately turned my thoughts to my new ambition. And yet the thing Maka had just told me kept coming back to my mind, and so it does to this very day. I know not why I should mention it at all save that each time I think upon Maka, I also think upon the lightning, whether I will or no.

I slept not at all that night, but sat* till the dawn came, thinking out a plan of action. By that time I was fair convinced that there was naught to be gained by waiting; waiting makes me impatient as well. I determined to act at once; and since one day is quite as good as the next, I decided that this day was to see the thing begun.

I came before the emperor at noon and received my decorations. Within the hour I had made myself known to the four and ninety men who were to be my command; a picked company, all of a height and weight, with bodies that lacked little of my own perfection. Never was there a finer guard about the palace.

My first care was to pick a quarrel with the outgoing commander. 'Twere easy enough; he was green with envy, anyhow. And so it came about that we met about mid afternoon, with seconds, in a well-frequented field in the outskirts.

Before supper was eaten my entire troop knew that their new captain had tossed his ball-slinger away without using it, had taken twenty balls from their former commander's weapon, and while thus wounded had charged the man and despatched him with bare hands! Needless to say, this exploit quite won their hearts; none but a blind man could have missed the respect they showed me when, all bandaged

---

*It seems to have been the custom among the soldiers never to lie down, but to take their sleep sitting or standing; a habit not hard to form where the gravitation was so slight. No doubt this also explains their stunted legs.

and sore, I lined them up next morning. Afterward I learned that they had all taken a pledge to "follow Strokor through the gates of Hofe itself!"

'Twere but a week later that, fully recovered and in perfect fettle, I called my men together one morn as the sun rose. By that time I had given them a sample of my brains through ordering a rearrangement of their quarters such as made the same much more comfortable. Also, I had dealt with one slight infraction of the rules in such a drastic fashion that they knew I would brook no trifling. All told, 'tis hard to say whether they thought the most of me or of Jon.

"Men," said I, as bluntly as I knew, "the emperor is an old man. And, as ye know, he is disposed to be lenient toward the men of Klow; whereas, ye and I well know that the louts are blackguards.

"Now, I will tell ye more. It has come to me lately that Klow is plotting to attack us with strange weapons." I thought best, considering their ignorance, not to give them my own reasons. "Of course I have told the emperor of it; yet he will not act. He says to wait till we are attacked."

I stopped and watched their faces. Sure enough; the idea fair made them ache. Each and every one of these men was spoiling for a fight.

"Now, tell me; how would ye like to become the emperor's body-guard?" I did not have to wait long; the light that flared in their faces told me plainly. "And—how would ye like to have me for your emperor?"

At that their tongues were loosed, and I hindered them not. They yelled for pure joy, and pressed about me like a pack of children. I saw that the time was ripe for action.

"Up, then!" I roared, and, of course, led the way. We met the emperor's guard on the lower stairs; and from that point on we fair hacked our way through.

Well, no need to describe the fight. For a time I thought we were gone; the guards had a cunningly devised labyrinth on the second floor, and attacked us from holes in a false ceiling, so that we suffered heavily at first. But I saw what was amiss, and shouted to my men to clear away the timbers;

52

and after that it was clear work. I lost forty men before the guard was disposed of. The emperor I finished myself; he dodged right spryly for a time, but at last I caught him and tossed him to the foot of the upper stairs. And there he still lies, for none of my men would touch him, nor would I. We covered him with quicklime and some earth.

As soon as we had taken care of those who were not too far gone, I called the men together and caused a round of spirits to be served. Then we all feasted on the emperor's store, and soon were feeling like ourselves.

"Men," I said impressively, "I am proud of ye. Never did an emperor have such a dangerous gang of bullies!"

At that they all grinned happily, and I added: "And 'tis a fine staff of generals that ye'll make!"

Need I say more? Those men would have overturned the palace for me had I said the word. As it was, they obeyed my next orders in such a spirit that success was assured from the first.

First, using the dead emperor's name, I caused the various chiefs to be brought together at once to the court chamber. At the same time I contrived, by means I need not go into here, to prevent any word of our action from getting abroad. So, when the former staff faced me the next morning, they learned that they were to be executed. I could trust not one; they were all friends of the old man.

With the chiefs out of the way, and my own men taking their commands, the whole army fell into my hands. True, there were some insurrections here and there; but my men handled them with such speed and harshness that any further stubbornness turned to admiration. By this time the fame of Strokor was spread throughout the empire.

And thus it came about that, within a week of the night that old Maka first put the idea into my head, Strokor, son of Strok, reigned throughout Vlamaland. And, to make it complete, the army celebrated my accession by taking a pledge before Jon:

"To Strokor, the fittest of the fit!"

IV

THE ASSAULT

Now, OUT OF A total population of perhaps three million, I had about a quarter-million first-class fighters in my half of the world. Klow, by comparison, had but two-thirds the number; his land was not a rich one.

But he had the advantage of knowing, some while in advance, of the new ruler in Vlama; and shortly my spies reported that his armories were devising a new type of weapon. 'Twas a strange verification of my own fiction to my men. I could learn nothing, however, about it.

Meanwhile I caused a vast number of flat-boats to be built, all in secret. Each of them was intended for a single fighter and his supplies; and each was so arranged, with side paddle wheels, that it would be driven by the motor in the soldier's chariot, and thus give each his own boat.

Again discarding all precedent, I packed not all my forces together, as had been done in the past, but scattered them up and adown the coast fronting the land of Klow; and at a prearranged time my quarter-million men set out, a company in each tiny fleet. Some were slightly in advance of the rest, who had the shorter distance to travel. And, just as I had planned, we all arrived at a certain spot on Klow's coast at practically the same hour, although two nights later.

'Twas a brilliant stroke. The enemy looked not for a fleet of water-ants, ready to step right out of the sea into battle. Their fleet was looking for us, true, but not in that shape. And we were all safely ashore before they had ceased to scour the seas for us.

I immediately placed my heavy machines, and just as all former expeditions had done, opened the assault at once with a shower of the poison shells. I relied, it will be seen, upon the surprise of my attack to strike terror into the hearts of the louts.

But apparently they were prepared for anything, no matter how rapid the attack. My bombardment had not proceeded many moments before, to my dismay, some of their own shells began to fall among us. Soon they were giving as good as we.

"Now, how knew they that we should come to this spot?" I demanded of Maka. I had placed him in my cabinet as soon as I had reached the throne.

The old man stroked his beard gravely. "Perchance it had been wrong to come to the old landing. They simply began shelling it as a matter of course."

"Ye are right again," I told him; and forthwith moved my pieces over into another triangle. (Previously, of course, all my charioteers had gone on toward the capital). However, I took care to move my machines, one at a time, so that there was no let-up in my bombardment.

But scarce had we taken up the new position before the enemy's shells likewise shifted, and began to strike once more in our midst. I swore a great oath and whirled upon Maka in wrath.

"Think ye that there be a spy among us?" I demanded. "How else can ye explain this thing? My men have combed the land about us; there are none of the louts secreted here; and, even so, they could not have notified Klow so soon. Besides, 'tis pitch dark." I were sorely mystified.

All we could do was to fling our shells as fast as our machines would work and dodge the enemy's hail as best we could. Thus the time passed, and it were near dawn when the first messengers* returned.

---

*Messengers; no telegraph or telephone, much less wireless. In a civilization as strenuous as that of Mercury, there was never enough consideration for others to lead to such socially beneficial things as these, no more than railroads or printing presses. Civilization appears to be in exact proportion to the ease of getting a living, other conditions being equal.

"They have stopped us just outside the walls of the city," was the report. It pleased me that they should have pushed so far at first; I climbed at once into my chariot.

"Now is the time for Strokor to strike!" I gave orders for the staff to remain where it was. "I will send ye word when the city is mine."

But before I started my engine I glanced up at the sky, to see if the dawn were yet come; and as I gazed I thought I saw something come between me and a star. I brushed the hair away from my eyes, and looked again. To my boundless surprise I made out, not one, but three strange objects moving about swiftly in the air!

"Look!" I cried, and my whole staff craned their necks. In a moment all had seen, and great was their wonder. I blamed them not for their fears.

'Twas Maka who spoke first. "They are much too large to be creatures of Jon," he muttered. "They must be some trick of the enemy.

"Dost recall Edam's vision of the creatures in the air of Jeos?" he went on, knowing that I would not hinder him. "Now, as I remember it, he said they flew with great speed. Were it not possible, Strokor, for suitable engines to propel very light structures at such high speed as to remain suspended in the air, after the manner of leaves in a storm? I note these strangers move quite fast."

It was even so; and at that same instant one of them swung directly above our heads, so close that I could hear the hum of a powerful engine. So it was only a trick! I shook myself together.

"Attention!" My staff drew up at the word. "They are but few; fear them not! We waste no more time here! Pack up the machines, and follow!"

And thus we charged upon Klow.

I found that my men had entirely surrounded the city. Klow's men were putting up a plucky fight, and showing no signs of fearing us. Seeing this, I blew a blast on my engine's whistle, so that my bullies might know that I had come.

Immediately the word ran up and down the line, so that

within a few minutes Klow was facing a roaring crowd of
half-mad terrors. I myself set the example by charging the
nearest group of the enemy, all of whom were mounted within
the rather small and perfectly circular chariots which they
preferred. They were quick, but slippery. Also, they could
not stand before a determined rush, as several of them learned
after vainly trying to slip some balls through my windows
and, failing in that, striving to get away from me.

But I ran them down, and toppled them over, and dropped
suffocation bombs into their little cages with such vigor and
disregard of their volleys that my men could not resist the
example. We charged all along that vast circular line, and
we cheered mightily when the whole front broke, turned tail,
and ran before us.

But scarce had they got away before a queer thing happened. A flock of those great air-creatures, some eight altogether, rose up from the middle of the city. It was now fairly
light, and we could see well. One of them had some sort of
engine trouble, so that it had to return at once; but the other
seven came out to the battle-line and began to circle the city.

As they did so they dropped odd, misshapen parcels, totally unlike materials of war; but when they struck they gave
off prodigious puffs of a greenish smoke, of so terribly pun-
gent a nature that my men dropped before it like apples
from a shaken tree. 'Twas a fearful sight; lucky for us that
the louts had had no practice, else few of us should be alive
to tell the tale.

And so they swept around the great circle, many triangles
in area; and everywhere the unthinkable things smote the
hearts of my men with a fear they had never known. Only
one of the devices suffered; it was brought down by a chance
fling of a poison shell. The rest, after loosing their burdens,
returned to the city for more.

I am no fool. I saw that we could do nothing against such
weapons, but must use all our wits if we escaped even.

"Return!" I commanded, and instantly my staff whistled
the code. The men obeyed with alacrity, making off at top

speed with the men of Klow in hot pursuit, although able to
do little damage.

Aye, it were a sorrowful thing, that retreat. The best I
could do was to remain till the very last, having to deal with
a number of persistent louts who all but suffocated me, at
that. But I managed to empty my slinger into some of them,
and to topple the rest. I was mainly angry that Klow had not
showed himself.

By the time I had reached the seashore, most of my men
were in their boats. Again I stayed till the last, although I
could see the enemy's fleet bearing down hard upon us from
the north. In truth we would have all been lost, had we
come in the manner of former campaigns, all together in big
transports. But because we could scatter every which way,
the fleet harmed us little; and four-fifths of us got safely back.

Happily, none of the air-machines had range enough to
reach Vlamaland. As soon as I could get my staff together, I
gave orders such as would insure discipline. Then, reminding
my hearties that Klow, knowing our helplessness, would
surely attack as soon as fully equipped, I made this offer:

"To the man who shall suggest the best way of meeting
their attack, I shall give the third of my empire!"

So they knew that the case was desperate. As for myself,
I slept not a bit, but paced my sleep-chamber and thought
deeply.

Now, a bit of a shell, from an enemy slinger, had pene-
trated my arm. Till now, I had paid no attention to it. But it
began to bother me, so I pulled the metal from my arm with
my teeth. And quite by chance I placed the billet on the
table within a few inches of the compass I had carried on my
boat.

To my intense surprise the needle of the compass swung
violently about, so that one end pointed directly at the frag-
ment of metal. I moved them closer together; there was no
doubt that they were strongly attracted. The enemy's shells
were made of mere iron!

The moment I fully realized this, I saw clearly how we
might baffle the men of Klow. I instantly summoned some

men, gave the orders much as though I had known for years what was to be done, and in a few moments had the satisfaction of seeing my messengers hurrying north and south.

And so it came about that, within three days of our shameful retreat, a tenth of my men were at work on the new project. As yet there was no word from my spies across the sea; but we worked with all possible haste. And this, very briefly, is what we did:

We laid a gigantic line of iron clear across the empire. From north to south, from snow to snow; one end was bedded in the island of Pathna, where the north magnetic-pole is found, while the other stopped on the opposite side of the world, in a hole dug through the ice into the solid earth of the South Polar Plain. And every foot of that enormous rod —'twas as big around as my leg—was insulated from the ground with pieces of our secret non-magnetic alloy!

Not for nothing had our chemists sought the metal which would resist the lightning. And not for nothing did my bullies piece the rod together, all working at the same time, so that the whole thing were complete in seven days. That is, complete save for the final connecting link; and that lay, a loglike roll of iron, at the door of my palace, ready to be rolled into place when I were but ready.

And on the morrow the Klow reached our shores.

V

THE VICTORY

MY FIRST INTENT was to let them advance unhampered; but Maka pointed out that such a policy might give them suspicions, and so we disputed their course all the way. I gave orders to show no great amount of resistance; and thus, the louts reached Vlama in high feather, confident that the game was theirs.

I stood at the door of the palace as Klow himself rolled up to the edge of the parade-ground. My men, obeying orders, had given way to him; his crews swarmed the space behind and on all sides of him, while my own bullies were all about and behind the palace. Never did two such giant armies face one another in peace; for I had caused my banner to be floated wrong end to, in token of surrender.

First, a small body of subordinates waited upon me, demanding that I give up the throne. I answered that I would treat with none save Klow himself; and shortly the knave, surrounded by perhaps fifty underlings, stepped up before me.

"Hail, Stroker!" he growled, his voice shaking a bit with excitement; not with fear, for he were a brave man. "Hail to thee and to thine, and a pleasant stay in Hofe for ye all!"

"Hail, Klow!" replied I, glancing up meaningly at the air monsters wheeling there. "I take it that ye purpose to execute us."

"Aye," he growled savagely. "Thou didst attack without provocation. Thy life is forfeit, and as many more as may be found needful to guarantee peace."

"Then," I quoth, my manner changing, "then ye have saved me the trouble of deciding what shall be thy fate. Execution, say you? So be it!"

And I strode down to the great log of iron which lay ready to fill the gap. Klow looked at me with a peculiar expression, as though he thought me mad. True, it looked it; how could I do him harm without myself suffering?

But I kicked the props which held the iron, and gave it a start with my foot. The ends of the pole-to-pole rod lay concealed by brush, perchance fifty yards away. In ten seconds that last section had rolled completely between them; and only a fool would have missed seeing that, the last ten feet, the iron was fair jerked through the air.

As this happened we all heard a tremendous crackling, like that of nearby lightning, while enormous clouds of dust arose from the two concealed ends, which were now become connections. And at the same time a loud, steely click, just one and no more, sounded from the intruding host.

For a moment Klow was vastly puzzled. Then he snarled

angrily: "What means this foolery, Strokor? Advance, and give up thy ax!"

For answer I turned me about, so as to face my men, and held up my hand in signal. Instantly the whistles sounded, and my hearties came bounding into the field.

"Treachery!" shouted Klow; and his officers ran here and there, shouting: "To arms! Charge and destroy! No quarter!"

But I paid little attention to the hubbub. I were gazing up at those infernal creatures of the air; and my heart sang within me as I saw them, circling erratically but very surely down to the earth. And as they came nearer, my satisfaction was entire; for their engines were silent!

At the same time consternation was reigning among our visitors. Not a man of all Klow's thousands was able to move his car or lift a weapon. Every slinger was jammed, as though frozen by invisible ice; all their balls and shells were stuck together, like the work of a transparent glue. Even their side arms were locked in their scabbards; and all their tugging could not budge them not!

But none of my men were so handicapped. Each man's chariot was running as though naught had happened; they thundered forward, discharging their balls and shells as freely as they had across the sea. Their charge was a murderous one; not a man of Klow's was able to resist, save with what force he could put into his bare hands.

Klow saw all this from the middle of his group of officers. None were able to more than place his body 'twixt us and their chief. In a very few moments they saw that the unknown magic had made them as children in our hands; they were utterly lost; and Klow turned away from the sight with a black face. Again he faced me.

"What means this, ye huge bundle of lies? What mean ye by tricking us with yon badge of surrender, only to tie our hands with thy magic of Hofe? Is this the way to fight like a man?"

I had stood at ease in my door since rolling the iron. Now, I looked about me still more easily; my men were running down the louts, who had jumped from their useless chariots and taken to their heels. 'Twere but a matter of time before the army of Klow would be no more, at that rate.

"Klow," I answered him mildly; "ye are right; this is not the way to fight like a man. Neither," I pointed out one of the fallen air-cars; "neither is that the way, flitting over our heads like shadows, and destroying us with filthy smoke! Shame on ye, Klow, for stooping to such! And upon thy own head be the blame for the trick I have played upon ye!"

"You attacked us without provocation," he muttered, sourly.

"Aye, and for a very good reason," I replied. "Yet I see thy viewpoint, and shalt give thee the benefit of the doubt." I turned to my whistlers and gave an order; so that presently the great slaughter had stopped. My men and Klow's alike struggled back to see what were amiss.

I handed Klow an ax. "Throw away thine own, scabbard and all," I told him. "It is useless, for 'tis made of iron. Ours, and all our tools of war, are formed of an alloy which is immune from the magic."

He took the ax in wonderment. "What means it, Strokor?" asked he again, meanwhile stripping himself in a businesslike fashion that it were good to see.

"It means," said I, throwing off my robe, "that I have unchained the magnetism of this world. Know you, Klow, that all of the children of the sun are full of his power; it is like unto that of the tiny magnet which ye give children for to play; but it is mighty, even as our world is mighty."

"Good Jon!" he gasped; for his was not a daring mind. "What have ye done, ye trifler?"

"I have transformed this empire into one vast magnet," I answered coolly. Then I showed him a boulder on the summit of a distant hill; through the tube, Klow could see some of my men standing beside it.

"Place one of thy own men on the roof of the palace," I told Klow, "and give him orders to lower my banner should ye give him the word.

"For upon the outcome of this fight 'twixt me and thee, Klow, hinges the whole affair! If thou dost survive, down comes my banner; and my men on the hill shall topple the

THE LORD OF DEATH

boulder, which shall rush down the slope and burst the iron
rod and break the spell. Stand, then, and defend thyself!"

And it did me good to see the spirit fly into his eyes. He
saw that his empire lived or died as he lived or died, and he
fought as he had never fought before. Small man that he
was, beside myself, he were wondrous quick and sure in his
motions; before I knew it, he had bit his ax deep into my
side.

And in another moment or two it was over. For, as soon as
I felt the pain of that gash, I flung my own blade away; and
with a roar such as would have shaken a stouter heart than
his, I charged the man, took a second fearful blow full on my
chest and heeding it not at all I snatched the ax from his
hands. Then, as he turned to run, I dropped that tool also.

And I ran him down, and felled him, and broke his head
with my hands.

VI*

THE FITTEST

SLAVES; but the most were slain. Neither could we bother
with their women and others left behind.

Now, by this time the empire was as one man in its wor-
ship of me. I had been emperor but a year, and already I
had made it certain that only the men of Vlamaland, and
no others, should live in the sight of Jon. So well thought
they of me, I might fair have sat upon my reputation, and
have spent my last days in feasting like the man before me.

But I was still too young and full of energy to take my

---

*This chapter was originally as long as the others, but an
unfortunate accident of Mr. Smith's, before he was thoroughly
familiar with the machine, mutilated a large portion of the
tape so badly that it was made worthless. This explains why
something appears to be missing from the account, and also
why this chapter begins in the middle of a sentence.

ease. I found myself more and more restless; I had naught to do; it had all been done. At last I sent for old Maka.

"Ye put me up to this, ye old fraud," I told him, pretending to be wrathful. "Now set me another task, or I'll have thy head!"

He knew me too well to be affrighted. He said that he had been considering my case of late.

"Strokor, thy father was right when he told thee to have naught to do with women. That is to say, he were right at the time. Were he alive today"—I forgot to say that my father was killed in the battle across the sea—"he would of a certainty say that it were high time for thee to pick thy mate.

"Remember, Strokor; great though thou art, yet when death taketh thee thy greatness is become a memory. Methinks ye should leave something more substantial behind."

It took but little thought to convince me that Maka were right once more. Fact; as soon as I thought upon it, it were a woman that I was restless for. The mere notion instantly gave me something worth while to look forward to.

"Jon bless thee!" I told the old man. "Ye have named both the trouble and the remedy. I will attend to it at once."

He sat thinking for some time longer. "Has thought of any woman in special, Strokor?" said he.

I had not. The idea was too new to me. "The best in the world shall be mine, of course," I told him. "But as for which one—hast any notion thyself?"

"Aye," he quoth. " 'Tis my own niece I have in mind. Perchance ye remember her; a pretty child, who was with me when thou didst save my life up there on the mountainside."

I recalled the chit fairly well. "But she were not a vigorous woman, Maka. Think you she is fit for me?"

"Aye, if any be," he replied earnestly. "Ave is not robust, true, but her muscles are as wires. It is because of what lies in her head, however, that I commend her. I have taught her all I know."

"So!" I exclaimed, much pleased. "Then she is indeed fit

to be the empress. And as I recall her, she were exceedingly good to look at."

"Say no more. Ave shall be the wife of Strokor!" And so it was arranged.

Well, and there ye have the story of Strokor, the mightiest man in the world, and the wisest. More than this I shall not tell with my own lips; I shall have singers recite my deeds until half the compartments in the House of Words is filled with the records thereof. But it were well that I should tell this much in mine own way.

My ambition is fulfilled. Let the hand of Jon descend upon our world, if it may; I care not if presently the sun come nearer, and the water dry up, and the days grow longer and longer, till the day and the year become of the same length. I care not; my people, such as be left of them, shall own what there is, and shall live as long as life is possible.

I shall leave behind no race of weaklings. Every man shall be fit to live, and the fittest of them all shall live the longer. And he, no matter how many cycles hence, shall look back to Strokor, and to Ave, his wife, and shall say:

"I am what I am, the last man on the world, because Strokor was the fittest man of his time!"

Aye; my fame shall live as long as there be life. Tonight, as I speak these things into the word machine, my heart is singing with the joy of it all. Thank Jon, I were born a man, not a woman!

Tomorrow I go to fetch Ave. I shall not send for her; I cannot trust her beauty to the hands of my crew. The more I think of her, the more I see that mine whole life hath been devised for this one moment. I see that, insignificant though she be, Ave is a needed link in the chain. I have come to want her more than food; I am become a lovesick fool!

Aye! I can afford to poke fun at myself. I can afford anything in this world; for I be its greatest man.

Its greatest man! Here is the place to stop. There is no more I can say, the story is done; the story of Strokor, the greatest man in the whole world!

VII

THE GOING

'TIS SEVERAL years since last I faced this machine, many and many a day since I said that my story was done, and placed the record on the shelf of my anteroom, my heart full of satisfaction. And today I must needs add another record, perhaps two, to the pile.

When I set out for the highlands on the morn following what I last related I took with me but two or three men; not that I had any need for guards, but because it looketh not well for the emperor to travel without retainers, however few. Practically, I was alone.

I reached the locality as the sun went down. The sky was a brilliant color; I remember it well. Darkness would come soon, though not as quickly as farther south. Commonly, I think not upon such trifles; but I were nearing my love, and tender things came easily to my mind.

My chariot kept to the road which lay alongside the irrigating flume, a stone trough which runs from the snow-covered hills to the dry country below. I had already noted this flume where it emptied into the basin in the valley below; for it had had a new kind of a spillway affixed to it, a broad, smooth platform with a slightly upward curve, over which the water was shooting. I saw no sense in the arrangement, and made up my mind to ask Maka about it; for the empire prized this trough most highly. It ran straight and true, over expensive bridges where needed, with scarce a bend to hold back the flow.

When I stopped my car outside the house I was surprised that none should come out to greet me. Maka had sent word of my coming; all should have been in readiness. But I was forced to use my whistle.

THE LORD OF DEATH

There was no stir. I became angry; I told my bullies to stay where they were, and myself burst in the door.

The house was a sturdy stone affair of one floor, set against the side of the mountain, a short distance above the flume. I looked about the interior in surprise; for not a soul was in sight in any of the compartments. There were signs that people had been there but a few moments before. I called it strange, for I had seen no one leave the house as I approached.

At last, as I was inspecting the eating place, I noted a small door let into the outer wall. It was open; and by squeezing I managed to get through. I found that it let into a long, dark passage.

I followed this, going steadily down a flight of stairs, and all of a sudden bumped into an iron grating. At the same moment I saw that the passageway made a turn just beyond; and by craning my neck and straining my eyes I could see a faintly lighted chamber just a few feet away

And before my eyes could scarce make out the figures of some people in the middle of the place, a voice came to my ear.

"Hail, Strokor!" it said; and great was my astonishment as I recognized the tones of Edam, the young dreamer whom Maka had brought to my house.

"Edam!" I cried. "What do ye here? Come and open these bars!"

He made no reply, save to laugh in a way I did not like. I shook the grating savagely, so that I felt it give. "Edam!" I roared. "Open this grating at once; and tell me, where is Ave?"

"I am here," came another voice; and I stopped in sheer surprise, to peer closer and to see, for the first time, that it were really the dreamer and the chit, these two and no more, who sat there in the underground chamber. They seemed to be sitting in some sort of a box, with glass windows.

"Ave—come here!" I spoke much more gently than to

Edam; for my heart was soft with thoughts of her. "It is thy lord, Strokor, the emperor, who calls thee. Come!"

"I stay here," said she in the same clear voice, entirely unshaken by my presence. "Edam hath claimed me, and I shall cleave to him. I want none of ye, ye giant!"

For a moment I was minded to throw my weight against the barrier, such was my rage. Then I thought better on it, and closely examined the bars. Two were loose.

"Ave," said I, contriving to keep my voice even, although my hands were busy with the bars as I spake. "Ave—ye do wrong to spite me thus. Know ye not that I am the emperor, and that these bars cannot stand before me? I warn ye, if I must call my men to help me, and to witness my shame, it will go hard with ye! Better that ye should come willingly. Ye are not for such as Edam."

"No?" quoth the young man, speaking up for the chit. "Ye are wrong, Strokor. We defy thee to do thy worst; we are prepared to flee from ye at all costs!"

I had twisted one of the bars out of my way without their seeing it. I strove at the next as I answered, still controlling my voice: "'Twill do ye no good to flee, Edam; ye know that. And as for Ave—she shall wish she had never been born!"

"So I should," she replied with spirit, "if I were to become thy woman. But know you, Strokor, that Ave, the daughter of Durok, would rather die than take the name of one who had spurned her, as ye did me!"

So I had; it had slipped my mind. "But I want thee now, Ave," said I softly, preparing to slip through the opening I had made. "Surely ye would not take thine own life?"

"Nay," she answered, with a laugh in her voice. "Rather I would go with Edam here. I would go," she finished, her voice rising in her excitement, "away from this horrible man's world; away from it all, Strokor, and to Jeos! Hear ye? To Jeos! And—"

But at that instant I burst through the grating. Without a sound I charged straight for the pair of them.

THE LORD OF DEATH

And without a sound they slipped away from before my grasp. Next second I was gazing stupidly at the rushing, swirling water of the flume.

And I saw that they had been sitting in the cabin of a tiny boat, and that they had got away!

There was an opening into the outer air; I rushed through, and stared in the growing twilight down the black furrow of the flume. Far in the distance, and going like a streak, I spied the glittering glass windows of the little craft. Once I made out the flutter of a saucy hand.

"We shall get them when they reach the valley!" I shouted to the men. Then I reached for my tube, and sighted it on the lower end of the flume, far, far below, almost too far away to be clear to the naked eye.

In an incredibly short time the craft reached the end. It traveled at an extraordinary rate; perchance 'twas weighted; I marveled that its windows could stand the force of the air. And I scarce had time to fear that the twain should be destroyed on that upturned spillway before it was there.

And then an awesome thing happened. As the boat struck the incline it shot upward into the air at a steep slant. Up, up it went; my heart jumped into my mouth; for surely they must be crushed when they came down.

But the craft did not come down. It went on and on, up and up; its speed scarcely slackened; 'twas like that of a shooting star. And in far less time than it takes to tell it, the little boat was high up among the stars, going higher every instant, and farther away from me. And suddenly the sweat broke cold on my forehead; for dead ahead, directly in line with their travel, lay the bluish white gleam of Jeos.

So great was my rage over the escape of the dreamer with my woman, at first I felt no sorrow. Later, after days and days of search in and about the basin, I came to grieve most terribly over my loss. When I came home to the palace, I was well-nigh ill.

In vain did I make the most generous of rewards. The whole empire turned out to search for the missing ones, but nothing came of it all. Yet I never ceased to hope, especially after my talk with Maka.

"Aye," he said, when I questioned him, "it were barely possible that they have left this world for all time. I have calculated the speed which their craft might have attained, had it the right proportions, and, in truth, it might have left the spillway at such a speed that it entirely overcame the draw of the ground.

"But I think it were a slim chance. It is more than likely, Strokor, that Ave shall return to thee."

Was I not the fitter man? Surely Edam's purpose could not succeed; Jon would not have it so. The woman was mine, because I had chosen her; and she must come back to me, and in safety, or I should tear Edam into bits.

But as time went on and naught transpired, I became more and more melancholy. Life became an empty thing; it had been empty enough before I had craved the girl, but now it was empty with hopelessness.

After a while I got to thinking of some of the things Maka had told me. The more I thought of the future, the blacker it seemed. True, there were many other women; but there had been only one Ave. No such beauty had ever graced this world before. And I knew I could be happy with no other.

Now I saw that all my fame had been in vain. I had lost the only woman that was fit for me, and when I died there would be naught left but my name. Even that the next emperor might blot out, if he chose. It had all been in vain!

"It shall not be!" I roared to myself, as I strode about my compartment, gnawing at my hands in my misery. And in just such a fit of helpless anger the great idea came to me.

No sooner conceived than put into practice. I will not go closely into details; I will relate just the outstanding facts. What I did was to select a very tall mountain, located almost on the equator, and proclaimed my intention to erect a monument to Jon upon its summit. I caused vast quanities of materials to be brought to the place; and for a year a hundred thousand men labored to put the pieces together.

When they had finished, they had made a mammoth tower, partly of wood and partly of alloy. It was made in sections, so that it might be placed, piece upon piece, one above another high into the sky.

It was an enormous task. When it was complete, I had a tower as high as the mountain itself erected upon its summit.

And next I caused section after section of the long, iron, pole-to-pole rod, which had tricked Klow, to be hauled up into the tower. I was only careful to begin the process from the top and work downward. I gave word that the last three sections be inserted at midday at a given day.

And at that hour I was safe inside a non-magnetic room.

I know right well when the deed was done. There was a most terrific earthquake. All about me, though I could see nothing at all, I could hear buildings falling. The din was appalling.

At the same time the air was fairly shattered with the rattle of the lightning. Never have I heard the like before. The rod had loosed the wrath of the forces above our air!

And as suddenly the whole deafening storm ended. Perchance the rod was destroyed by the lightning; I never went to see. For I know, the electricity split the very ground apart. But I gazed out of a window in the top of my palace, and saw that I had succeeded.

Not a soul but myself remained alive.

None but buildings made of the alloy were standing. Not only man, but most of his works had perished in that awful blast. I, alone, remained!

I, Strokor, am the survivor! I, the greatest man; it were but fit that I should be the last! No man shall come after me, to honor me or not as he chooses. I, and no other, shall be the last man!

And when Ave returns—as she must, though it be ages hence—when she comes, she shall find me waiting. I, Strokor, the mighty and wise, shall be here when she returns. I shall wait for her forever; here I shall always stay. The stars may move from their places, but I shall not go!

THE LORD OF DEATH

For it is my intention to make use of another secret Maka taught me. In brief—*

PART III

THE SURVIVOR

PROVIDED WITH a sledge-hammer, a crowbar, and a hydraulic jack, and even with drills and explosives as a last resort, Jackson, Kinney, and Van Emmon returned the same day to the walled-in room in the top of that mystifying mansion. The materials they carried would have made considerable of a load had not Smith removed enough of the weights from their suits to offset their burden. They reached the unopened door without special exertion, and with no mishap.

They looked in vain for a crack big enough to hold the point of the crowbar; neither could the most vigorous jabbing loosen any of the material. They dropped that tool and tried the sledge. It got no results; even in the hands of the husky geologist, the most vigorous blows failed to budge the door. They did not even dent it.

So they propped the powerful hydraulic jack, a tool sturdy enough to lift a house, at an angle against the door. Then, using the crowbar as a lever, the architect steadily turned up the screw, the mechanism multiplying his very ordinary strength a hundredfold. In a moment it could be seen that he was getting results; the door began to stir. Van Emmon struck one edge with the sledge-hammer, and it gave slightly.

In another minute the whole door, weighing over a ton, had been pushed almost out of its opening. The jack over-

---

*The record ends here. It may be that Strokor left the machine for some trivial reason, and forgot to finish his story. At all events, it is necessary to refer to the further discoveries of the expedition in order to learn the outcome of it all.

balanced, toppled over; they did not readjust it, but threw their combined weight upon the barrier.

There was no need to try again. With a shiver the huge slab of metal slid, upright, into the space beyond, stood straight on end for a second or so, then toppled to the floor. *And this time they heard the crash.*

For, as the door fell, a great gust of wind rushed out with a hissing shriek, almost overbalancing the men from the earth. They stood still for a while, breathing hard from their exertion, trying in vain to peer into the blackness before them. Under no circumstances would either of them have admitted that he was gathering courage.

In a minute the architect, his eyes sparkling with his enthusiasm for the antique, picked up the electric torch and turned it into the compartment. As he did so the other two stepped to his side, so that the three of them faced the unknown together. It was just as well. Outlined in that circle of light, and not six feet in front of them, stood a great chair upon a wide platform; and seated in it, erect and alert, his wide open eyes staring straight into those of the three, was the frightful mountainous form of Strokor, the giant, *himself.*

For an indeterminable length of time the men from the earth stood there, speechless, unbreathing, staring at that awful monster as though at a nightmare. He did not move; he was entirely at ease, and yet plainly on guard, glaring at them with an air of conscious superiority which held them powerless. Instinctively they knew that the all-dominating voice in the records had belonged to this Hercules. But their instinct could not tell them whether the man still lived.

It was the doctor's brain that worked first. Automatically, from a lifelong habit of diagnosis, he inspected that dreadful figure quite as though it were that of a patient. Bit by bit his subconscious mind pieced together the evidence; the man in the chair showed no signs of life. And after a while the doctor's conscious mind also knew.

"He is dead," he said positively, in his natural voice; and such was the vast relief of the other two that they were in no way startled by the sound. Instantly all three drew long

73

breaths; the tension was relaxed; and Van Emmon's curiosity found a harsh and unsteady voice.

"How under heaven has he been preserved all this time? Especially," he added, remembering, "considering the air that we found in the room?"

The doctor answered after a moment, his reply taking the form of advancing a step or two and holding out a hand. It touched glass.

For the first time since the discovery, the builder shifted the light. He had held it as still as death for a full minute. Now he flashed it all about the place, and they saw that the huge figure was entirely encased in glass. The cabinet measured about six feet on each of its sides, and about five feet in height; but such were the squat proportions of the occupant that he filled the whole space.

A slight examination showed that the case was not fixed to the platform, but had a separate bottom, upon which the stumplike chair was set. Also, they found that, thanks to the reduced pull of the planet, it was not hard for the three of them to lift the cabinet bodily, despite its weight of almost a thousand pounds. They left the tools lie there, discarded as much weight as they could, and proceeded to carry that ages-old superman out into the light.

Here they could see that the great man was all but a negro in color. It was equally clear, however, from an examination of his mammoth cranium and extraordinary expression, that he was as highly developed along most mental lines as the greatest men on earth. It was the back of his head, however, so flat that it was only a continuation of his neck, or, rather, shoulders, that told where the flaw lay. That, together with the hardness of his eye, the cruelty of his mouth, and the absolute lack of softness anywhere in the ironlike face or frame—all this condemned the monster for what he was; inhuman.

It was not easy to get him down the two flights of stairs. More than once they had to prop the case on a step while they rested; and at one time, just before they reached that curious heap of rubbish at the foot of the upper stairs,

74

THE LORD OF DEATH

Jackson's strength gave way and it looked as though the whole thing would get away from them. Van Emmon saved it at the cost of a bruised shoulder.

Once at the bottom of the lower flight, the rest was easy. Within a very few minutes the astonished face of the engineer was peering into the vestibule; he could hardly wait until the air-tight door was locked before opening the inner valves. He stared at the mammoth figure in the case long and hard, and from then on showed a great deal of respect for his three friends.

Of course, at that time the members of the expedition did not understand the conditions of Mercury as they are now known. They had to depend upon the general impression they got from their first-hand investigations; and it is remarkable that the doctor should have guessed so close to the truth.

"He must have made up his mind to outlast everybody else," was the way he put it as he kicked off his suit. He stepped up to the cabinet and felt of the glass. "I wish it were possible, without breaking the case, to see how he was embalmed."

His fingers still rested on the glass. Suddenly his eyes narrowed; he ran his fingers over the entire surface of the pane, and then whirled to stare at a thermometer.

"That's mighty curious!" he ejaculated. "This thing was bitter cold when we brought it in! Now it's already as warm as this car!"

Smith's eyes lit up. "It may be," he offered, "that the case doesn't contain a vacuum, but some gas which has an electrical affinity for our atmosphere."

"Or," exclaimed the geologist suddenly, "the glass itself may be totally different from ours. It may be made of—"

"God!" shouted the doctor, jerking his hand from the cabinet and leaping straight backward. At the same instant, with a grinding crash, all three sides of the case collapsed and fell in splinters to the floor.

"Look out!" shrieked Jackson. He was staring straight into the now unhooded eyes of the giant. He backed away, stumbled against a stool, and fell to the floor in a dead faint. Smith fumbled impotently with a hammer. The doctor was shaking like a leaf.

But Van Emmon stood still in his tracks, his eyes fixed on the Goliath; his fingernails gashed the palms of his hands, but he would not budge. And as he stared he saw, from first to last, the whole ghastly change that came, after billions of years of waiting, to the sole survivor of Mercury.

A glaze swept over the huge figure. Next instant every line in that adamant frame lost its strength; the hardness left the eyes and mouth. The head seemed to sink lower into the massive shoulders, and the irresistible hands relaxed. In another second the thing that had once been as iron had become as rubber.

But only for an instant. Second by second that huge mountain of muscle slipped and jellied and actually melted before the eyes of the humans. At the same time a curious acrid odor arose; Smith fell to coughing. The doctor turned on more oxygen.

In less than half a minute the man who had once conquered a planet was reduced to a steaming mound of brownish paste. As it sank to the floor of the case, it touched a layer of coarse yellow powder sprinkled there; and it was this that caused the vapor. In a moment the room was filled with the haze of it; luckily, the doctor's apparatus worked well.

And thus it came about that, within five minutes from being exposed to the air of the sky-car, that whole immense bulk, chair and all, had vanished. The powder had turned it to vapor, and the purifying chemicals had sucked it up. Nothing was left save a heap of smoking, grayish ashes in the center of the broken glass.

Van Emmon's fingers relaxed their grip. He stirred to action, and turned briskly to Smith.

"Here! Help me with this thing!"

Between them they got the remains of the cabinet, with its gruesome load, into the vestibule. As for the doctor, he was bending over Jackson's still unconscious form. When he saw what the others were doing, he gave a great sigh of relief.

"Good!" He helped them close the door. "Let's get away from this damned place!"

The outer door was opened. At the same time Smith started the machinery; and as the sky-car shot away from the ground he tilted it slightly, so that the contents of the vestibule was slid into space. Down it fell like so much lead.

The doctor glanced through a nearby window, and his face brightened as he made out the distant gleam of another planet. He watched the receding surface of Mercury with positive delight.

"Nice place to get away from," he commented. "And now, my friends, for Venus, and then—home!"

But the other's eyes were fixed upon a tiny sparkle in the dust outside the palace, where the vestibule had dropped its load. It was the sun shining upon some broken bits of glass; the glass which, for untold ages, had enclosed the throne of the Death-lord.

THE QUEEN OF LIFE

I

NEXT STOP, VENUS!

WHEN HE FIRST got the idea of the sky-car, the doctor never stopped to consider whether he was the right man for such an excursion. Personally, he hated travel. He was merely a general practitioner, with a great fondness for astronomy; and the sole reason why he wanted to visit the planets was that he couldn't see them well enough with his telescope. So he dabbled a little in magnetism and so forth, and stumbled upon the principle of the cube.

But he had no mechanical ability, and was on the point of giving up the scheme when he met Smith. He was instantly impressed by the engineer's highly commonplace face; he had had considerable experience with human contrariness, and felt sure that Smith must be an absolute wonder, since he looked so very ordinary.

Kinney's diagnosis proved correct. Smith knew his business; the machinery was finished in a hurry and done right.

However, when it came to fitting the outfit into a suitable sky-car, Kinney was obliged to call in an architect. That accounts for E. Williams Jackson. At the same time, it occurred to the doctor that they would need a cook. Mrs. Kinney had refused to have anything whatever to do with the trip, and so Kinney put an ad in the paper. As luck would have it, Van Emmon, the geologist, who had learned how to cook when he first became a mountaineer, saw the ad and answered it in hope of adventure.

The doctor himself, besides his training in the mental and bodily frailities of human beings, had also an unusual command of the related sciences, such as biology. Smith's specialties have already been named; he could drive an airplane or a nail with equal ease. Van Emmon, as a part of his profession, was a skilled "fossilologist," and was well up in natural history.

As for E. Williams Jackson—the architect was also the sociologist of the four. Moreover, he had quite a reputation as an amateur antiquarian. Nevertheless, the most important thing about E. Williams Jackson was not learned until after the visit to Mercury, after the terrible end of that exploration, after the architect, falling in a faint, had been revived under the doctor's care.

"Gentlemen," said Kinney, coming from the secluded nook among the dynamos which had been the architect's bunk; "gentlemen, I must inform you that Jackson is not what we thought.

"He—I mean, she—is a woman!"

Which put an entirely new face upon matters. The three men, discussing it, marveled that the architect had been able to keep her sex a secret all the time they were exploring at Mercury. They did not know that none of E. Williams Jackson's fellow architects had ever guessed the truth. Ambitious and ingenious, with a natural liking for house-planning, she had resolved that her sex should not stand in the way of success.

And when she finally came to herself, there in her bunk, and suspected that her secret was out—instead of shame or

embarrassment she felt only chagrin. She walked, rather un-
steadily, across the floor of the great cube-shaped car to the
window where the three were standing; and as they quietly
made a place for her, she took it entirely as a matter of
course, and without a word.

The doctor had been speaking of the peculiar fitness of the
four for what they were doing. "And if I'm not mistaken," he
went on, "we're going to need all the brains we can pool,
when we get to Venus.

"I never would have claimed, when we started out, that
Mercury had ever been inhabited. But now that we've seen
what we've seen, I feel dead sure that Venus once was peo-
pled."

The four looked out the triple-glazed vacuum-insulated
window at the steadily growing globe of "Earth's twin sister."
Half in sunlight and half in shadow, this planet, for ages the
synonym for beauty, was now but a million miles away. She
looked as large as the moon; but instead of a silvery gleam,
she showed a creamy radiance fully three times as bright.

"Let's see," reflected the geologist aloud. "As I recall it,
the brightness of a planet depends upon the amount of its air.
That would indicate, then, that Venus has about as much as
the earth, wouldn't it?" remembering how the home planet
had looked when they left it.

The doctor nodded. "There are other factors; but undoubtedly we are approaching a world which is a great deal
like our own. Venus is nearly as large as the earth, has about
nine-tenths the surface, and a gravity almost as strong. The
main difference is that she's only two-thirds as far from the
sun as we are."

"How long is her day?" Smith wanted to know.

"Can't say. Some observers claim to have seen her clearly
enough to announce a day of the same length as ours. Others
calculate that she's like Mercury; always the same face toward the sun. If so, her day is also her year—two hundred
and twenty-five of our days."

Van Emmon looked disappointed. "In that case she
would be blistering hot on one side and freezing cold on the

other; except," remembering Mercury, "except for the 'twilight zone,' where the climate would be neither one nor the other, but temperate." He pointed to the line down the middle of the disk before them, the line which divided the lighted from the unlighted, the day from the night.

The four looked more intently. It should be remembered that the very brilliance of Venus has always hindered the astronomers; the planet as a whole is always very conspicuous, but its very glare makes it impossible to see any details. The surface has always seemed to be covered by a veil of hazy, faintly streaked vapor.

Smith gave a queer exclamation. For a moment or two he stared hard at the planet; then looked up with an apologetic grin.

"I had a foolish idea. I thought—" He checked himself. "Say, doesn't Venus remind you of something?"

The doctor slowly shook his head. "Can't say that it does, Smith. I have always considered Venus as having an appearance peculiarly her own. Why?"

The engineer started to answer, stopped, thought better of it, and instead pointed out the half that was in shadow. "Why is it that we can make out the black portion so easily?"

Kinney could answer this. "The fact is, it isn't really black at all, but faintly lighted. Presumably it is star-shine."

"Star-shine!" echoed the architect, interested.

"Just that. You see," finished the doctor, "if that side is never turned toward the sun, then it must be covered with ice, which would reflect the star—"

"Ah!" exclaimed Smith with satisfaction. "I wasn't so crazy after all! My notion was that the whole blamed thing is covered with ice!"

It looked reasonable. Certainly the entire sphere had a somewhat watery appearance. It prompted the geologist to say:

"Kinney—if that reflection is really due to ice, then there must be plenty of water vapor in the air. And if that's the case—"

"Not only is life entirely possible," stated the doctor

81

quietly, "but I'll bet you this sky-car against an abandoned soap-stone mine that we find humans, or near-human beings there when we land tomorrow!"

II

SPEAKING OF VENUS

THE ARCHITECT WAS still dressed in the fashionably cut suit of men's clothes she had worn while in the car. Van Emmon thought of this when he said, somewhat awkwardly:

"Well, I'm going to fix something to eat. It'll be ready in half an hour, Miss—er—Jackson."

She looked at him, slightly puzzled; then understood. "You mean to give me time to change my clothes? Thanks; but I'm used to these. And besides," with spirit, "I never could see why women couldn't wear what they choose, so long as it is decent."

There was no denying that hers were both becoming and "decent." Modeled after the usual riding costume, both coat and breeches were youthfully, rather than mannishly, tailored; and the narrow, vertical stripe of the dark gray material served to make her slenderness almost girlish. In short, what with her poet-style hair, her independent manner and direct speech, she was far more like a boy of twenty than a woman nearing thirty.

She walked with Van Emmon, dodging machinery all the way, across the big car to the little kitchenette over which he had presided. There, to his dismay, the girl took off her coat, rolled up her sleeves, and announced her intention of helping.

"You're a good cook, Van—I mean, Mr.—"

"Let it go at Van, please," said he hastily. "My first name is Gustave, but nobody has ever used it since I was christened."

"Same with my 'Edna,'" she declared. "Mother's name was Williams, and I was nicknamed 'Billie' before I can remember. So that's settled," with great firmness. "The point is—Van—you're a good cook, but everything tastes of bacon. I wish you'd let me boss this meal."

He looked rebellious for an instant, then gave a sigh of relief. "I'm really tickled to death."

A little later the doctor and Smith, looking across, saw Van Emmon being initiated into the system which constructs scalloped potatoes. Next, he was discovering that there is more than one way to prepare dried beef.

"For once, we won't cream it," said E. Billie Jackson, dryly, as Van Emmon laid down the can-opener. "We'll make an omelet out of it, and see if anything happens."

She was already beating the eggs. He cut up the meat into small pieces, and when he was finished, took the egg-beater away from her. He turned it so energetically that a speck of foam flew into his face.

"Go slow," she advised, nonchalantly reaching up with a dish-towel and wiping the fleck away. Whereupon he worked the machine more furiously than ever.

Soon he was wondering how on earth he had come to assume, all along, that she was not a woman. He now saw that what he had previously considered boyishness in her was, in fact, simply the vigor and freshness of an earnest, healthy, energetic girl. It dawned upon him that her keen, gray eyes were not sharp, but alert; her mouth, not hard, but resolute; her whole expression, instead of mannish, just as womanly as that of any girl who has been thrown upon her own resources, and made good. He soon found that his eyesight did not suffer in any way because he looked at her.

"Now," she remarked, in her businesslike way, as she placed the brimming pan into the oven, "I suppose that I'll hear various hints to the effect that a woman has no business trying to do men's stunts. And I warn you right now that I'm prepared to put up a warm argument!"

"Of course," said the geologist, with such gravity that the girl knew he didn't mean it; "of course a woman's place is in the home. Surrounded by seventeen or eighteen children, and cooking for that many more hired men besides, she is simply ideal. We realize that."

"Then, admitting that much, why shouldn't a woman be as independent as she likes? Think what women did during the war; remember what a lot of women are doctors and lawyers! Is there any good reason why I couldn't design a library as well as a man could?"

"None at all," agreed Van Emmon, handing over the dish of chopped meat. The girl carefully folded the contents into the now spongelike omelet as he went on: "By the way, a neighbor of mine told me, just before I left, that he was having trouble with a broken sewer. How'd you like to—"

"About as well as you'd like to darn socks!" she came back, evidently being primed for such comments. She took a look at the potatoes, and then permitted the geologist to open their sixth can of peaches. "I must say they're good," she admitted, as she noted the eagerness with which he obeyed.

Bread and butter, olives, coffee and cake completed that meal. The table was set with more care than usual, a clean cloth and napkins being unearthed for the occasion. When Smith and Kinney were called, both declared that they weren't hungry enough to do justice to it all.

"It's just as well you weren't very hungry," commented Billie, as she finished giving each of them a second helping of the potatoes. "There's barely enough left for me," and she took it.

"Say, I never thought of it before, Miss—er—Miss Billie," said Smith coloring; "but you eat just as much as a man!"

"Ye gods, how shocking!" she jeered. "Come to think of it, Smith, you eat *more* than a woman!"

The doctor's face grew red with some suppressed emotion. After a while he said soberly: "I'll tell you what's worrying Smith. He's afraid that women, having suddenly become very progressive, will forge entirely ahead of men. You understand —having started, they can't stop. And I must admit that I've thought seriously of it at times myself."

"Me too," added Van Emmon earnestly. "I have the same feeling about it that an elderly man must have when he sees a young one get on the job. Instead of being glad that the women are making good, I sort of resent it."

"I knew it!" exclaimed the girl delightedly. "But I never heard a man admit it before!"

"Perhaps it isn't as serious as we think," said the practical Smith, scraping the bottom of the potato pan. "I believe that the progress of women may have a fine effect upon men, making us less self-satisfied, and more alert. For one thing," glancing about the cube, "we've got to clean up a bit, now that we know you're a woman!"

The architect's eyes flashed. "Because you know mighty well I'll light in and do it myself, if you don't; that's what you mean! Please take notice that I'm to be respected, not because of what I *am*, but because of what I can *do!*"

"In behalf of myself and companions, I surrender!" said the doctor gallantly. Then he instantly added: "And yet, even when we are actually chivalrous, we are disregarding your desire to be appreciated for what you are worth. Pardon me, Miss Billie; I'll not forget again.

"At the same time, my dear," remembering that he had a daughter of his own, nearly the builder's age, "we men have come to think of women primarily as potential mothers, and secondarily as people of affairs. And considering that motherhood is something that is denied to us lords of the earth—"

"For which we can thank a merciful Providence," interjected the girl solemnly.

"Considering this—excuse my seriousness—really amazing fact, you can't blame us for expecting women to fulfil this vital function before taking up other matters."

"Yes?" remarked the girl, watching the peaches with anxious eye as Ven Emmon helped himself. "Funny; but I always understood that the first function of man was to father the race; yet, invariably the young fellows try to make names for themselves before, not after, they marry!"

"Scalped!" chuckled Van Emmon, as the doctor hid his discomfiture behind a large piece of cake. "You may know a lot about Venus, doc, but you don't know much about women!"

THE QUEEN OF LIFE

"Speaking about Venus," Smith was reminded, "we may learn something bearing upon the very point we have been discussing if Kinney's right about the inhabitants."

The doctor nodded eagerly. "You see, if there's people still alive on the planet, they're probably further advanced than we on the earth. Other things being equal, of course. Being a smaller planet than ours, she cooled off sooner, and thus became fit for life earlier. And having been made from the same 'batch,' to use Van's expression, that Mercury and all the rest were, why, in all likelihood evolution has taken place there much the same as with us, only sooner.

"I should expect," he elaborated largely, "that we shall find the inhabitants much the same as we humans, only extremely civilized. It may be that they are as far above us as we are above monkeys."

Smith broke in by quoting an astronomer who contended that Venus kept only one face toward the sun. "Maybe she always did, Kinney."

The doctor shook his head. "See how perfectly round she is? No oblateness whatever. It proves that she once revolved, otherwise she'd be pear-shaped, from the sun's pull."

There was a short silence, during which Billie concluded that the only scraps left would be the coffee-grounds. Then Van Emmon pushed away from the table, got to his feet, stretched a little to relieve his nerves, and said:

"Well, whatever we find on Venus, I hope the women do the cooking!"

III

THE FIRST VENUSIAN

WHEN THE sky-car was within a thousand miles of the surface, Smith adjusted the currents so that the floor was directed downward. The four changed from the window to the deadlight, and watched the approaching disk with every

86

bit of the excitement and interest they had felt when nearing Mercury.

The doctor had warned them that the heavy atmosphere which Venus was known to possess would prevent seeing as clearly as in the case of the smaller planet. All were much disappointed, however, to find that they were still unable to make out a single definite detail. The great half-shining, half-black world showed nothing but that vaguely streaked, ice-like haze.

There was something very queer about it all. "Strange that we should see no movement in those clouds," mused the doctor aloud. "That is, if they really are clouds."

Van Emmon already doubted it. "Just what I was thinking. There ought to be terrific winds; yet, so far as I have seen, there's been nothing doing anywhere on the surface since we first began to observe it."

After a while the doctor put away his binoculars and rubbed his eyes. "We might as well descend faster, Smith. Can't see a thing from here."

Unhindered by air to impede its progress the sky-car had been hurtling through space at cometary speed. Now, however, Smith added the power of the apparatus to the pull of the planet, so that the disk began to rush toward them at a truly alarming rate. After a few seconds of it Billie found herself unconsciously moving to the side of the geologist.

He looked down at her, understood, and flushed with pleasure. "There's no danger," he confidently assured her, with the result that, her courage fortified, the girl moved back to her place again. Van Emmon inwardly kicked himself.

So deceptive was that peculiar fogginess Smith throttled their descent as soon as they had reached the point where the planet's appearance changed from round to flat. They were headed for the line which marked the boundary of the shadow. This gray "twilight zone" was three or four hundred miles in width; on the right of it—to the east—the dazzling surface of that sunlit vapor contrasted sharply with the all

87

but black mistiness of the starward side. Clearly the zone ought to be temperate enough.

Down they sank. As they came nearer a curious pinkish tint began to show beneath them. Shortly it became more noticeable; the doctor gave a sudden grunt of satisfaction, and Smith stopped the car.

A minute later the doctor had taken a sample of the surrounding ether through his laboratory test-vestibule; and shortly announced that they were now floating in air instead of space.

"Good deal like ours back home, too"—exultingly. "Pretty thin, of course." He made a short calculation, referring to the aneroid barometer which was mounted on the outer frame of a window, and said he judged that their altitude was about five miles.

The descent continued, Smith using the utmost caution. The other three kept their eyes glued to the deadlight; and their mystification was only equaled by their uneasiness as that motionless, bleary glaze failed absolutely to show anything they had not seen a thousand miles higher. Not a single detail!

"It reminds me," said the girl in a low voice, "of something I once saw from the top of a hill. It was the reflection of the sun from the surface of a pond; not clear water, but covered with—"

"Good Heavens!" interrupted Van Emmon, struck with the thought. "Can it be that the whole planet is under water?"

Beyond a doubt his guess was justified. There was an oily smoothness about that dazzling haze which made it remarkably like a lake of still and rather dirty water under a bright sun.

But the doctor said no. "Any water I ever heard of would make clouds," said he; "and we know there's air enough to guarantee plenty of wind. Yet nothing seems to be in motion." He was frowning continually now.

It was Billie who first declared that she saw the surface. "Stop," she said to Smith evenly, and he instantly obeyed. All four gathered around the deadlight, and soon agreed that the peculiarly elusive skin of the planet was actually within sight. However, it was like deciding upon the distance of the moon—as easy to say that it were within arm's reach as a long ways off.

The doctor went to a window. There he could look out upon the sun, a painfully bright object much larger than it looks from the Earth. It was just "ascending," and half of it was below the horizon. A blinding streak of light was reflected from a point on the surface not far from the cube. Shading his eyes with his hand the doctor could see that the mysterious crust was absolutely smooth.

On the opposite side of the car the horizon ended in a sunrise glow of a slightly greenish radiance. From that side the pinkish tint of the surface was quite pronounced.

Before going any lower the doctor, struck with an idea, declared: "We always want to remember that this car is perfectly soundproof. Suppose we open the outer door of the vestibule. I imagine we'll learn something peculiar."

It was possible to open this door without touching the inner valves, using mechanism concealed within the walls. The moment it was done—the door faced the "north"—pandemonium itself broke loose. A most terrific shrieking and howling came from the outside; it was wind, passing at a rate such as would make a hurricane seem a mere zephyr. The doctor closed the door so that they could think.

"It's the draft," he concluded; "the draft from the sun-warmed side to the cold side."

As for Van Emmon, he was getting out a rope and a heavy leaden weight. On the rope he formed knots every five feet, about twenty of them; and after getting into one of the insulated, aluminum-armored and oxygen-helmeted suits with which they had explored Mercury, he locked himself on the other side of the inner vestibule door and proceeded to "sound."

To the amazement of all except Billie "bottom" was reached in less than twenty feet. "I thought so," she said with satisfaction; but she was not at ease until Van Emmon had returned in safety from that booming, whistling turmoil.

His first remark upon removing his helmet almost took them off their feet. "The point is," said he, throttling his excitement—"the point is, the rope was nearly jerked out of my hands!

"Understand what I mean? The surface is *revolving!*"

This upset every idea they had had; it never occurred to any of them that the planet could revolve at such speed that it would appear stationary. Smith went at once to the eastern window and watched closely, for fear some irregularity in that apparently perfect sphere might catch them unawares. They did not learn till later that Venus's day is a little less than twenty-five hours, and therefore, since they had approached her near the equator, the wind they had encountered was moving at nearly nine hundred miles per hour!

Bit by bit, though, the cube answered to the wind-pressure. Soon they noted the sun rising slowly; and by the time it was two hours high the surface, which had been whizzing under them like some highly polished top, became entirely motionless: The cube had "stopped."

One minute later the car touched the level. Smith very slowly reduced the repelling current so that the immense weight of the cube was but gradually shifted to the unknown surface beneath. Ton after ton was added until—

"Stop!" came from the doctor. He had noted through the window a slight curvature in the material.

So the machinery was left in action. "At any rate," said Smith, "we know that the confounded stuff isn't antimagnetic, whatever it is." Of course this was true—even though the gelatinlike shell could not support the cube's weight, yet it did not insulate the planet from the repelling current.

The thermometer registered three hundred and thirty-five degrees Fahrenheit. "Two hundred and eighty degrees higher than it would be at home in the same latitude," remarked the doctor. "We'll have to use the suits." He took it for granted that exploration should begin at once.

No one stayed behind. The machines could be relied upon, as they knew from nearly two weeks of use, and certainly there was nothing in sight which could possibly interfere with the cube. Nevertheless, the matter-of-fact engineer took care to remove part of the door-operating apparatus when he left the vestibule, and nobody commented upon it. It seemed the sensible thing to do; that was all.

There was just about enough additional weight in their suits to balance the slightly reduced gravitation, so they moved about, four misshapen, metallic hulks, with as much freedom as though back home. Always they kept within a few feet of each other so as to throw no strain on their interconnecting telephone wires. The big, glass-faced helmets gave a remarkable sense of security.

They made a complete circuit of the cube, and at the end of it looked at each other in perplexity. Never, save in the middle of an ocean, in the doldrums, did any man ever see such a totally barren spot. Not a tree, much less a sign of human occupation; there was not even the slightest mound. The planet was, in actual fact, as smooth and as bare as a billiard ball!

Moreover, the surface itself remained as mysterious as before. Of course they did not touch it with bare hands—all wore insulated mittens—but the dazzling stuff was certainly as hard as steel and as highly polished. It was neither transparent nor opaque, but translucent, "like pink mother-of-pearl," as Billie suggested.

She was the first to propose that they move to another spot. "We ought to try a place where it's not yet dawn," said she, shielding her eyes from the glare. (It will be remembered that the suits protected them from the heat itself.) "Can't see anything."

"Hush!" hissed the doctor. They turned and followed his gaze to a spot not thirty feet from where they stood.

At the same instant they felt a faint jar in the material under their feet. And next second they saw that a large section of the supposedly solid surface was in motion.

A portion about ten feet square was being lifted bodily in front of their eyes, and before another word was said this block of the unknown substance was raised until they could see that it was all of a yard thick. Up it went at the same deliberate rate; and the four involuntarily moved closer together as they saw that there was something underneath.

It was a cage, for all the world like that of an elevator, except that it was made of clear glass. Another second and it had stopped, with its floor level with the surface; and the people from the earth saw that it contained a man.

He was quite tall, slenderly built, and dressed in a queer satiny material which fitted him like an acrobat's suit. He was extremely thin as to legs, narrow as to shoulders, deep in the chest and short in the waist. All this, however, they saw after their inspection of his head.

It was human! Marvelously refined in every detail, yet it was set upon a graceful neck, and modeled upon much the same lines as that of any man. It was not that of a brute, nor yet that of a bird; it was—human!

He stood at ease, resting slightly on one foot, and dispelled any notion that he might be unreal by shifting his weight occasionally. Meanwhile he watched the four with a grave, interested smile; and they, in turn, came closer.

His chin was small, even retreating; but his mouth was wide and curved into an exaggerated Cupid's bow. Even as he continued to smile the curves did not leave his lips; they, however, were thin rather than thick. His nose was quite small, with a decidedly Irish cast; but his eyes, set far apart above quite shallow cheekbones, were exceedingly large and of a brilliant blue. In fact, it was mainly his eyes that gave character to his face; although none could overlook his breadth of forehead, running back to a cranium that fairly bulged over the ears, and seemed ready to rise like a tightly inflated balloon. His skin was pure white.

And so they stood for uncounted minutes. At last the doctor noted that the stranger was eying them with far less interest than they showed in him; he stood as though he felt on display; and the doctor gave an exclamation of perplexity that broke the spell. The four impulsively drew up to the glass; Van Emmon touched it with his mitten; and that is how the four explorers came to receive the vibrations that came next.

For the man in the cage, in turn, put out his hand and touched the glass opposite Van Emmon. Then he opened his mouth.

"I am very glad to see you," said he in a soft, pulsating voice—and in the best of English.

IV

A PUZZLED WORLD

FOR A MOMENT blank amazement gripped the four. Then amazement gave way to genuine apprehension. Were they insane to imagine that this man of another world had spoken to them in their own language? Each looked at the other, and was astounded to see that all had heard the same thing.

Presently the stranger spoke again; if anything, the kindly smile on his face became even broader. "Suppose we postpone explaining how I am able to use your tongue. It will be easier for you to understand after you have been with us a while." He spoke slowly and carefully, yet with a faint lisp, much as some infant prodigy might speak.

But there was no doubt that he had really done it. The doctor managed to clear his throat.

"You are right," said he, with vastly less assurance than the amazing stranger. "We will try to understand things in the order you think best to present them. You—should know best."

Kinney introduced himself by name and profession, also the other three. The stranger nodded affably to each. "You may call me Estra," said he, pronouncing it "Ethtra." "There is no occupation on the Earth corresponding with mine, but in my spare moments I am an astronomer like yourself."

The doctor silently marveled. He had not told the stranger about his hobby. Meanwhile the architect attempted to break the ice even finer.

93

"We take it for granted," said she rather nervously, "that your people are somewhat further advanced than us on the earth. However, we expect to be given credit for having visited your planet before you visited ours!" She said this with an engaging smile which won an instant response; the Venusian's lips almost lost their curves in his generous effort.

"You will find that we greatly respect all that you have accomplished," he declared earnestly. "As for your apparatus" —glancing at the cube—"you have the advantage on the earth of certain chemical elements which are entirely lacking here, otherwise we should have called upon you long ago."

He slipped a panel of glass to one side. "Step in quickly!" he exclaimed, gasping; and the four obeyed him without thought. It was only when the panel was replaced that they noticed the floor of the cage; it was of clear glass, like the sides, and looked totally incapable of bearing their combined weight.

The Venusian smiled at Smith's worried look. "The material is amply strong enough," said he. "I am only concerned about your machine there. Is it safe to be left alone?"

"So far as we know, yes," answered Van Emmon, who did not feel quite as much confidence in the stranger as the rest.

"Then we can go down at once." With these words the man in satin turned to a small black box in one wall of the elevator and touched a button.*

Instantly the car began to descend, at first slowly and then with swiftly increasing velocity. By the time the explorers had accustomed their eyes to the sudden semi-darkness, the cage was dropping at such a speed that the air fairly sang past its sides.

Far overhead was a square, black shadow in the waxlike crust which they had left; it was the shadow of the cube. All about them was a dimly lit network of braces, arches and

---

*For details of this and other matters of an electrical and mechanical nature, the technical reader is referred to Mr. Smith's reports to the A. S. M. E.

semitransparent columns; to all appearances the system seemed to support the crust. Billie whirled upon the Venusian:

"I've got it now! The whole globe is covered with glass!"

Estra smiled his approval. "For thousands upon thousands
of centuries, my friend. The thing was done when our ances-
tors first suspected that our planet was doomed to come so
near the sun. It was the only way we could protect ourselves
from the heat."

"Great!" exploded the doctor, admiration overcoming regret that he had not thought of it himself. But Smith had
other thoughts:

"How long did it take to finish the job? And what did it
cost?"

"Two centuries; and about twice the cost of your last war.
I need only suggest to you that we colored the material so
as to reflect most of the heat. That is why the material looks
blue from below, although pink from above."

"Say"—from Billie—"how long are we to keep on dropping like this?"

"We will arrive in a moment or two," answered the smiling
one. "The roof is raised several miles above the sea-level in
order to cover all the mountains."

By this time the four were able to make out things pretty
well. They saw that the dimness was only relative; the Venusian world was actually as well lighted as any part of the
earth on a cloudy day. And they saw that they were des-
cending in a locality of astonishing beauty.

The stranger halted the car so that they could inspect the
scene as though from an airplane. In no way did the landscape resemble that of the earth. To begin with, pillars of
huge dimensions were placed every quarter-mile or so; it
was these that supported the intricate archwork above. They
were made of the same translucent stuff as the crust, but had
a light topaz tint. The Venusian said:

"You will not need to be told that the science of metal-
lurgy has advanced quite far with us. All our metals can be
made transparent, if we like; those pillars are colored vari-

95

ously in different regions so as to be clearly distinguishable and prevent collisions of flying apparatus."

But Van Emmon and Billie were both more interested in what lay between the columns. They scarcely noticed that there were no people in sight at the time. The ground was covered with an indescribable wealth of color; and it was only by a close examination that the buildings could be distinguished as such.

For they were all made of that semi-transparent stuff. Of every conceivable tint and shade, the structure showed an utter lack of uniformity in size, shape or arrangement. Moreover, the ground was absolutely packed with them; they spread as far as the eye could reach.

But if there was profusion, there also was confusion— apparently. Streets ran anywhere and everywhere; there was no visible system to anything. And where there was no space for a building, invariably there was a shrub, a bush or a small tree of some kind, all in full flower. The only sign of regularity to be seen was in the roofs—practically all of them were flat. Whether the building was some rambling, loosely gathered agglomeration of vari-colored wings, or a single, towering skyscraper of one tint, almost inevitably it was crowned with a perfectly level surface.

"I see," said Van Emmon, thoughtfully. "You have no rain."

"Precisely"—from Estra. "We have the air completely under our control. We give our vegetation artificial showers when we think it should have it, not when nature wills; and similarly we use electricity instead of sunlight that we may stimulate its growth."

"In short"—Van Emmon put it as the car slid slowly down the remaining distance—"in short, you have abolished the weather."

The Venusian nodded. "And I'll save you the trouble of suggesting," he added, "that we are nothing more nor less than hothouse people!"

96

V

THE HUMAN CONSERVATORY

"But there is this difference," he cautioned as they stepped out of the elevator into a sort of a plaza, "that, whereas you people on the earth have only begun to use the hothouse principle, we here have perfected it.

"I suggest that you waste no time looking for faults."

Van Emmon stared at the doctor. "How does this idea fit your theory, Kinney—that Venus is simply the earth plus several thousand extra generations of civilization?"

"Fit?" echoed the doctor. "Fits like a glove. We humans are fast becoming a race of indoor-people despite all the various 'back-to-nature' movements. Look at the popularity of inclosed automobiles, for example.

"The only thing that surprises me"—turning to their guide —"is that you use your legs for their original purpose."

Estra smiled, and pointed out something standing a few feet away. It was a small, shuttle-shaped air-craft, with clear glass sides which had actually made them overlook it at first. Peering closer they saw that the plaza and surrounding streets were nearly filled with these all but invisible cars.

The Venusian explained. "You marvel that I use my legs and walk the same as you do. I am glad you have brought up this point, because it is a fact that our people use mechanisms instead of bodily energy, almost altogether. These cars you see are universally used for transportation. I am one of the very few who appreciate the value of natural exercise."

"Do you mean to say," demanded Van Emmon, "that the average Venusian does no walking?"

"Not a mile a year," said Estra gravely.

"Just what he is obliged to do indoors from room to room." And he involuntarily glanced down at his own extremely thin legs.

The architect's eyes widened with a growing understand-

97

ing. "I see now," she murmured. "That's why there was no one else to greet us."

The Venusian smiled gratefully. "We thought it best. You'd have been shocked outright, I am sure, had you been introduced to a representative Venusian without any explanation."

They fell silent. Still, without moving from the point where they had left the elevator, the four from the earth examined the surrounding buildings in a renewed effort to see some system in their arrangement. Directly in front of them was a particularly large structure. Like all the rest, it was of hopelessly irregular design, yet it had a large domed central portion which gave it the appearance of an auditorium; and the effect was further borne out by a subdued humming sound which seemed to come from it.

Smith asked Estra if it were a hall.

"Yes and no," was the answer. "It fills the purpose of a hall, but is not built on the hall plan." And Smith tried to stare through the translucent walls of the thing.

The other buildings within immediate reach were of every possible appearance. Some would have passed for cottages, others for stores, still others for the most fanciful of studios. And nowhere was there such a thing as a sign, even at the street corners, much less on a building.

"Not that we would be able to read your signs, if you had them," commented the doctor, "but I'd like to know how your people find their way without something of that kind to guide them."

Estra's smile did not change. "That is something you will understand better before long," said he, "provided you feel ready to explore a little further."

The four looked at each other in question, and suddenly it struck them all that they were a rather pugnacious-looking crew in their cumbersome suits of armor and formidable helmets. The doctor turned to Estra.

"You ought to know"—he appealed—"whether we can take off these suits now."

"It would be best," was the reply. "You will find the air

98

and temperature decidedly more warm and moist than what you have been used to, but otherwise practically the same. There is a slightly larger proportion of oxygen; that is all. Just imagine you are in a hothouse."

Smith and the doctor were already discarding their suits. Van Emmon and Billie followed more slowly; the one, because he did not share the doctor's confidence in their guide; the other, because of a sudden shyness in his presence. The Venusian noted this.

"You need not feel any embarrassment," said he to Billie's vast astonishment. "There is no distinction here between the dress of the two sexes." And again all four marveled that he should know so much about them.

Once out of the armor the visitors felt much more at ease. The slightly reduced gravitation gave them a sense of lightness and freedom which more than balanced the junglelike oppressiveness of the air. They found themselves guarding against a certain exuberance; perhaps it was the extra oxygen, too.

They strode toward the large structure directly ahead. At its entrance—a wide, square portal which opened into a fan-shaped lobby—Estra paused and smiled apologetically as he mopped his forehead and upper lip with a paper handkerchief, which he immediately dropped into a small, trap-covered opening in the wall at his side.

These little doors, by the way, were to be seen at frequent intervals wherever they went. Incidentally not a scrap of paper or other refuse was to be noted anywhere—streets and all were spotless.

As for Estra—"I am not accustomed to moving at such speed," he explained his discomfort. "If you do not mind, please walk a little more leisurely."

They took their time about passing through this lobby. For one thing, Estra said there would have to be a small delay; and for another, the walls and ceilings of the space were most remarkably ornamented. They were fairly covered with what appeared, at first glance, to be absolutely lifelike paintings and sculptures. They were so arranged as to strengthen

99

the structural lines of the place, and, of course, they were of more interest to Billie than to the others.*

Desiring to examine some of the work far overhead, Billie clambered up on a convenient pedestal in order to look more closely. She took the strength of things for granted, and put her weight too heavily on a molding on the edge of the pedestal; with the result that there was a sharp crack; and the girl struck the floor in a heap. She got to her feet before Van Emmon could reach her side, but her face was white with pain.

"Sprained—ankle," said she between set lips, and proceeded to stump up and down the lobby, "to limber up," as she said, although her three companions offered to do anything that might relieve her.

To the surprise of all, Estra leaned against a pillar and watched the whole affair with perfect composure. He made no offer of help, said nothing whatever in sympathy. In a moment he noticed the looks they gave him—their stares.

"I must beg your pardon," he said, still smiling. "I am sorry this happened; it will not be easy to explain.

"But you will find all Venusians very unsympathetic. Not that we are hard hearted, but because we simply lost the power of sympathy.

"We do not know what pity is. We have eliminated everything that is disagreeable, all that is painful, from our lives to such an extent that there is never any cause for pity."

The three young people could say nothing in answer. The doctor, however, spoke thoughtfully:

"Perhaps it is superfluous; but—tell me—have you done away with injustice, Estra?"

"That is just the point," agreed the Venusian. "Justice took the place of pity and mercy; it was so long ago I am barely able to appreciate your own views on the subject."

Billie, her ankle somewhat better, turned to examine other

---

*The specialist in architecture and related subjects is referred to E. Williams Jackson's report to the A. I. A., for details of these basrelief photographs.

work; but at the moment another Venusian approached from the upper end of the lobby. Walking slowly, he carried four small parcels with a great deal of effort, and the explorers had time to scrutinize him closely.

He was built much like Estra, but shorter, and with a little more flesh about the torso. His forehead bulged directly over his eyes, instead of above his ears, as did Estra's; also his eyes were smaller and not as far apart. His whole expression was equally kind and affable, despite a curiously shriveled appearance of his lips; they made the front of his mouth quite flat, and served to take attention away from his pitifully thin legs.

Estra greeted him with a cheery phrase, in a language decidedly different from any the explorers were familiar with. In a way, it was Spanish, or, rather, the pure Castilian tongue; but it seemed to be devoid of dental consonants. It was very agreeable to listen to.

Estra, however, had taken the four parcels from his comrade, and now presented him to the four, saying that his name was Kalara, and that he was a machinist. "He cannot use your tongue," said the Venusian. "Few of us have mastered it. There are difficulties.

"As for these machines"—unwrapping the parcels—"I must apologize in advance for certain defects in their design. I invented them under pressure, so to speak, having to perfect the whole idea in the rather short time that has elapsed since you, doctor, began the sky-car."

"And what is the purpose of the machines?" from Billie, as she was about to accept the first of the devices from the Venusian.

For some reason he appeared to be especially interested in the girl, and addressed half of his remarks to her; and it was while his smiling gaze was fixed upon her eyes that he gave the answer:

"They are to serve"—very carefully—"partly as lexicons and partly as grammars. In short, they are mechanical interpreters."

VI

THE TRANSLATING MACHINES

"First, let me remind you," said the Venusian, "of our lack of certain elements that you are familiar with on the Earth. We have never been able to improve on the common telephone. That is why we must still assemble in person whenever we have any collective activity; while on the Earth the time will come when your wireless principle will be developed to the point of transmitting both light and sound; and after that there will be little need of gatherings of any sort."

Then he explained the apparatus. It consisted of a miniature head-telephone, connected to a small, metallic case the size of a cigar-box, the cover of which was a transparent diaphragm. Estra did not open the case, but showed the mechanism through the cover.

"Essentially, this is a 'word-for-word' device," said he, pointing to a swiftly revolving dial within the box. "On one face of that dial are some ten thousand word-images, made by vibration, after the phonograph method. Directly opposite, on the other face, are the corresponding words in the other language. The disk is rotating at such an enormous speed that, for all practical purposes, any word which may chance to be spoken will be translated almost instantaneously."

He indicated two delicate, many-tentacled "feelers," as he called them, one on each face of the disk. One of these "felt" the proper word-image as it whirled beneath, while the other established an electrical contact with the corresponding waves beneath, at the same time exciting a complicated-looking talking machine.

"That," commented Estra, "is not so easy to explain. It transforms this literal translation into an idiomatic one. Perhaps you will understand its workings a little later when you learn how and why I am able to use your own language."

By this time the four had reached the point where nothing could surprise them. They were becoming accustomed to the unaccustomed. Had they been told that the Venusians had abolished speech altogether, they would have felt disappointed, but not incredulous. However, the doctor thought of something.

"Have you any extra 'records,' to be used in case we visit some other nations while we are here?"

For just a second the Venusian was puzzled; then his smile broadened. "The one record will do," said he, "wherever you go."

"A universal language!" Billie's eyes sparkled with interest.

"Long, long ago," Estra said. "It was established soon after our league of nations was formed."

"Does the league actually prevent war and promote peace?" demanded Van Emmon. This had been a disputed question when the four left the earth.

"We no longer have a league of nations," said their guide slowly. And instantly the four were eying him eagerly. This was really refreshing, to find that the Venusians were actually lacking in something.

"So it didn't work?" commented the doctor, disappointed.

But the Venusian's smile was still there. "It worked itself out," said he. "We have no further use for a league. We have no more nations. We are now—one."

And he helped them adjust the machines.

The cases were slung over their shoulders and the telephones clamped to their ears. When all ready, Estra began to talk, and his voice came nearly as sharp and clear through the apparatus as before. It was modified by a metallic flatness, together with a certain amount of mechanical noise in which a peculiar hissing was the most noticeable. Otherwise he said:

"I am now using my own language. If I make any mistakes, you must not blame the machine. It is as nearly perfect as I was able to make it."

He then asked them what blunders they noted. Billie, who was the most enthusiastic about the thing, declared that they

103

would have no trouble in understanding; whereupon Estra quietly asked:

"Do you feel like going now to try them out?"

Once more an exchange of glances between the four from the earth. Clearly the Venusians were extremely considerate people, to leave their visitors in the care of the one man, apparently, who was able to make them feel at home. There seemed to be no reason for uneasiness.

But Van Emmon still had his old misgivings about Estra. There was something about the effeminate Venusian which irritated the big geologist; it always does make a strong man suspicious to see a weaker one show such self-confidence. Van Emmon drew the doctor and Billie aside, while Smith and Estra went on with the test. Said Van Emmon:

"It just occurred to me that the cube might look pretty good to these people. You remember what this chap said about their lack of some of our chemicals. What do you think—is it really safe to put ourselves entirely in their power?"

"You mean," said the doctor slowly, "that they might try to keep us here rather than lose the cube?"

Van Emmon nodded gravely, but Billie had strong objections. "Estra doesn't look like that sort," she declared vehemently.

"He's too good natured to be a crook; he needs a guardian rather than a warden."

It flashed into the doctor's mind that many a woman had fallen in love with a man merely because he seemed to be in need of some one to take care of him.

That is, the self-reliant kind of woman; and Billie certainly was self-reliant. Something of the same notion came vaguely to the geologist at the same time; and with a vigor that was quite uncalled for, he urged:

"I say, 'safety first.' We shouldn't have left the cube unguarded. I propose that one of us, at least, return to the surface while the others attend this meeting—or trap, for all we know."

THE QUEEN OF LIFE

"All right," said Billie promptly. "Get Estra to show you how to use the elevator, and wait for us in the vestibule."

Van Emmon's face flamed. "That isn't what I meant!" hotly. "If anybody goes to the cube, it should be you, Billie!"

If Billie did not notice the use of her nickname, at least the doctor did. The girl simply snorted.

"If you think for one second that I'm going to back out just because I'm a woman, let me tell you that you're very badly mistaken!"

Van Emmon turned to the doctor appealingly, but the doctor took the action personally. He shook his head. "I wouldn't miss this for anything, Van. Estra looks safe to me. Go and ask Smith; maybe he is willing to be the goat."

The geologist took one good look at the engineer's absorbed, unquestioning manner as he listened to the Venusian, and gave up the idea with a sigh. For a moment he was sour; then he smiled shyly.

"I'm more than anxious to meet the bunch myself," he admitted; and led the way back to Estra. The Venusian looked at him with no change of expression, although there was something very disconcerting in the precocious wisdom of his eyes. Their very kindliness and serenity gave him an appearance of superiority, such as only aggravated the geologist's suspicions.

But there was nothing to do but to trust him. They followed him through two sets of doors, which slid noiselessly open before them in response to some mechanism operated by the Venusian's steps. This brought them to another of the glass elevators, in which they descended perhaps ten feet, stepping out of it onto a moving platform; this, in turn, extended the length of a low dimly lighted passageway about a hundred yards long. When they got off, they were standing in a small anteroom.

The Venusian paused and smiled at the four again. "Do you feel like going on display now?" he asked; then added: "I should have said: 'Do you feel like seeing Venus on display, for we all know more or less about you already.' "

But the visitors were braced for the experience. Estra

105

looked at each approvingly, and then did something which made them wonder. He stood stock still for perhaps a second, his eyes closed as though listening; and then, without explanation, he led the way through an opal-glass door into a brilliantly lighted space.

Next moment the explorers were standing in the midst of the people of Venus.

VII

THE ULTIMATE RACE

THE FOUR WERE at the bottom of a huge, conelike pit, such as instantly reminded the doctor of a medical clinic. The space where they stood was, perhaps, twenty feet in diameter, while the walls enclosing the whole hall were many hundreds of feet apart. And sloping up from the center, on all sides, was tier upon tier of the most extraordinary seats in all creation.

For each and every one of those thousands of Venusians was separately enclosed in glass. Nowhere was there a figure to be seen who was not installed in one of those small, transparent boxes, just large enough for a single person. Moreover—and it came somewhat as a shock to the four when they noted it—the central platform itself was both covered and surrounded with the same material.

"Make yourselves at home," Estra was saying. He pointed to several microphones within easy reach. "These are provided with my translators, so when you are ready to open up conversation, go right ahead as though you were among your own people." And he made himself comfortable in a saddlelike chair, as much as to say that there was no hurry.

For a long time the explorers stood taking it in. The Venusians, without exception, stared back at them with nearly equal curiosity. And despite the extraordinary nature of the proceeding, this mutual scrutiny took place in comparative silence; for while the glass gave a certain sense of security to the newcomers, it also cut off all sound except that low humming.

The nearest row of the people got their closest attention. Without exception, they had the same general build as Estra; slim, delicate, and anemic, they resembled a "ward full of convalescent consumptives," as the doctor commented under his breath. Not one of them would ever give a joke-smith material for a fat-man anecdote; at the same time there was nothing feverish, nervous, or broken down in their appearance. "A pretty lot of invalids," as Billie added to the doctor's remark.

Many observers would have been struck, first, by the extreme diversity in the matter of dress. All wore skin-tight clothing, and much of it was silky, like Estra's. But there was a bewildering assortment of colors, and the most extraordinary decorations, or, rather, ornaments. So far as dress went, there was no telling anything whatever about sex.

"Are they all men?" asked Billie, wondering, of Estra. The Venusian shook his head with his invariable smile. "Nor all women either," said he enigmatically.

But in many respects they were astonishingly alike. Almost to a soul their upper lips were withered and flat. One and all had short, emaciated-looking legs. Each and every one had a crop of really luxuriant hair; the shades varied between the usual blonde and brunette, with little of the reddishness so common on the earth; but there were no bald people at all. On the other hand, there were no beards or mustaches in the whole crowd; every face was bare!

"Like a lot of Chinamen," said Van Emmon in an undertone; "can't tell one from another." But Billie pointed out that this was not strictly true; a close inspection of the faces showed an extremely wide range of distinction. No two chins in the crowd were exactly alike, although not one of them showed any of the resolute firmness which is admired on the Earth. All were weak, yet different.

Neither were there any prominent noses, although there were none that could have been called insignificant. And while every pair of eyes in the place was large, as large as Estra's, yet there was every desirable color and expression.

To sum it all up, and to use the doctor's words: "They've developed a standard type, all right, just as the characteristic American face is the standard Earth type; but—did you ever see such variations?"

Nevertheless, the most striking thing about these people to the eyes of the visitors was their mutual resemblance. For one thing, there seemed to be no nervous people present. There were many children in the crowd, too; yet all sat very still, and only an occasional movement of the hands served to indicate consciousness. In this sense, they were all remarkably well bred.

In another, they were remarkably rude. At any given moment a good half of the people were eating, or, rather, sipping liquids of various sorts from small tumblers. Probably every person in the house, before the affair was over, had imbibed two or three ounces of fluid; but not once was the matter apologized for, nor the four invited to partake.

"So this may be the outcome of our outrageous habit of eating sweetmeats at theaters," muttered the doctor. And again noting the hairless faces: "Just what I said when men first began using those depilatories instead of shaving—no more beards!"

But it was Billie who explained the invariable crop of hair. "No use to look for baldness; they don't wear hats! Why should they, since there's neither sun nor rain to protect their heads from?"

Mainly, however, the architect was interested in the building itself. To her, the most striking feature was not the tremendously arched dome, nor yet the remarkable system of bracing which dispensed with any columns in all that vast space. It was something simpler—there were no aisles.

"Now, what do you make of that?" the girl asked Van Emmon. "How do they ever get to their places?" But he could not suggest anything more than to recall an individual elevator scheme once proposed.

To Smith, one object of interest was the telephone system.

Remarkably like those used on the Earth, one was located in each of the tiny glass cages. He was likewise puzzled to account for the ventilation system; each cage was apparently air-tight, yet no Venusian showed any discomfort.

But the geologist, for want of anything strictly within his professional range, interested himself in trying to fathom the moral attitude of these people. He was still suspicious of them, notwithstanding a growing tendency to like every one of their pleasant, really agreeable faces. There was neither solemnity, sourness, nor bitterness to be seen anywhere; at the same time, there was no sign of levity. In every countenance was the same inexplicable mixture of wisdom and benevolence that distinguished Estra. Nowhere was there hostility, and nowhere was there crudity. Somehow, the big geologist would have felt more at home had he seen something antagonistic. Essentially, Van Emmon was a fighter.

At last the four felt their attention lagging. Novelties always pall quickly, no matter how striking. Estra sensed the feeling and inquired:

"Which of you will do the honors?"

Instinctively the three younger folk turned to the doctor. He made no protest, but stepped at once to one of the microphones, put on his most impressive professional face, and began:

"My friends"—and Van Emmon noted a pleased look come into every face about them—"my friends, I do not need to state how significant this meeting is to us all. From what Estra has said, I gather that you have informed yourselves regarding us, in some manner which he has promised to make clear. At all events, I am exceedingly anxious to see your astronomical apparatus."

At this a broad smile came to many of the faces before him; but he went on, unnoticing: "Certainly there is not much I could tell you which you do not already know; Estra's use of our language proves this. I only need to assure you that we will be glad to answer any questions that may occur to you. It goes without saying that we, of course, are filled with delight to find your planet so wondrously and happily populated, especially after our experience on Mercury, of which, I presume, you are informed."

Apparently they were. The doctor went on: "You may be sure that we are fairly bursting with questions. However, we are content to become informed as Estra sees fit to guide us.

"There is just one thing, more than any other, which I would like to know at this time. Why is it that, although you all show a great lack of exercise, and are continually eating, you never appear to be healthy?"

Instantly a Venusian in the fifth row, to the doctor's right, touched his phone and replied: "It is a matter of diet. We have nothing but 'absolute' foods; if you understand what that means."

And from that time on, despite the fact that the explorers asked questions which, at home, would have found hundreds ready and able to answer, on Venus only one person answered any given question, and always without any apparent prearrangement. For a long time they could not account for this.

The doctor motioned for Smith to take his place. The engineer looked a little embarrassed, but cleared his throat noisily and said:

"I am especially struck with the fact that each of you sits in a separate glass pew, or case. Why is this?"

The reply came from one of the few people present who showed any signs of age. He was, perhaps, sixty, and his hair was fast whitening. He said:

"For reasons of sanitation. It is not wise to breathe the breath of another."

"Also," supplemented someone from the other side of that vast pit—"also, each is thereby enabled to surround himself with the electrical influences which suit him best."

Smith stepped back, pondering. The doctor looked to the geologist to take his place, but Van Emmon made way for Billie. At any other time she would have resented his "woman-first" attitude; now she quickly found voice.

"How are you able to get along without aisles? It may seem a foolish question, to you; but on earth we would consider a hall without aisles about as convenient as a room without a door."

Immediately a Venusian directly in front of her, and on a level with her eyes, called out: "Watch me, madam." And quite without an effort beyond touching a button or two, the fellow rose straight into the air, glass and all, and then floated gently over toward the middle of the hall.

"It probably appears complicated to you," explained the Venusian whose side he had just left. "We make use of elements not found on your earth."

Billie's *sang froid* was not shaken. Instantly she came back energetically: "Apparently your method overcomes gravitation. Why haven't you tried to travel away from your planet?"

And she looked around with the air of one who has uttered a poser, only to have another of the satin-clad people reply, from a point which she was not able to locate:

"Because enough such power cannot be safely concentrated."

As Billie retired, Van Emmon noted with growing irritation that the continuously affable aspect of the Venusians had not altered in any way, unless it was to become even more genial and sure. The big man strode energetically to the microphone, and the other three noted a general movement of interest and admiration as the people inspected him.

"Why," demanded he, "do we see no signs of contention? If you are familiar with conditions on the earth, you surely know that rivalry, in one form or another, is the accepted basis of life. But all of you, here, appear to be perfectly happy, and at the same time entirely sure of yourselves.

"We have just come from a planet where we have seen the principle of combat, of competition, carried so far that it seems to have wrecked the race; so you will pardon my curiosity, I am sure. From your faces, one would conclude that you had abolished self-interest altogether. Just why are you so—well, extraordinarily self-complacent?" And he thrust out his aggressive jaw as though to make up for the lack of chins about him.

"Because there is nothing for us to combat, save within

111

ourselves." This from a wide-faced chap in a bluish-white suit.

"But surely you have rivalry of some sort?"

"No." Another voice added: "Rivalry is the outgrowth of getting a livelihood; on earth it is inevitable, because men do the work. Here, everything is done by machines." Still another put in: "Discontent is the mother of ambition, but we are all content, because each possesses all he desires."

But the geologist was far from satisfied. "Then," said he vigorously, "if you have eliminated all contention, you have nullified the great law of contrasts. You say you are all rich. How do you know, if you have no poverty to contrast it with?

"On earth, we appreciate warmth because we have experienced cold; pleasure, because we know pain; happiness, because we have always had misery with us. If we have not had the one, we cannot value the other.

"If you have never been discontented, how do you know that you are content?"

VIII

THE KEY-NOTE

FOR A MINUTE or two it looked as though Van Emmon had raised an unanswerable question. There was no immediate reply. Even Estra looked around, as though in wonder at the silence, and seemed on the point of answering of his own accord when a voice came from a man far up on the left. He said:

"A little explanation may be wise. To begin with, you will agree that black is black because white is white; but it doesn't follow that blue is blue because green is green, or red is red. Blue is blue because it is neither green nor red nor any other color. It is blue, not because it contrasts with these other colors, but because it merely differs from them.

"Now, we on Venus do not need poverty, in order to ap-

112

THE QUEEN OF LIFE

preciate wealth. Instead, each of us is blessed with his own particular choice of wealth. Each is blessed in a different way; some with children, some with intellect, some with other matters; and the question of mere quantity never enters."

"We do not need pain or misery," spoke up someone else, "any more than you people on the earth require an additional color, in order to appreciate the variety you already have." And then, from a Venusian with an especially strong voice:

"That we are really content, we know absolutely. For each of us, in his own distinctive way, is wholly and peculiarly satisfied."

And it only added to the geologist's irritation to have these striking statements made in a good-humored, impersonal fashion which totally disarmed all opposition. That the Venusians were perfectly sure of their ground, was undeniable; but they had such a cheerful way of looking at it, as though they didn't care a rap whether Van Emmon agreed or not, that— If they'd only have shown some spirit! Van Emmon would have liked it infinitely better if one of them had only become hot about it.

At this point Estra rose in his chair. "I think you had best approach us from a fresh viewpoint," said he in his unfailingly agreeable manner. The doctor nodded vigorously, and again Estra closed his eyes in that odd, hesitating way. Immediately every one in the place, with the exception of a single person in the lowest row, took flight in his or her little glass pew. In a moment the great vault overhead was fairly swarming with people; and in less than a minute the last of them had floated out through one of the arches in the walls.

Estra opened a panel in the central cage, and admitted the Venusian who had stayed behind. She—for it appeared to be a young woman—walked with about the same facility as Estra; but as soon as she had entered the space, took the seat Estra had vacated, and waited.

The action rather disappointed the doctor. He removed the interpreting telephone from his head, and asked:

"I rather thought we were going to meet one of your officials, Estra. We'd hate to go back home without having

113

met your president, or whatever you call your chief executive."

The two Venusians exchanged smiles, and to the surprise of the explorers the woman gave the reply, in language as good as Estra's, but an even sweeter expression: "There is no such thing as a chief executive on Venus, friends."

"I meant," explained the doctor, rattled, "the chairman of your cabinet, or council, or whatever it is that regulates your affairs. Perhaps," with an inspiration, "I should have said, the speaker of your congress."

The Venusian shook her head, still smiling. She hesitated while selecting the best words; and the four noted that, while her features were quite as delicate as Estra's, her face was proportionately larger, and her whole figure better filled out. No one would have said that she was pretty, much less beautiful; but none would deny that she was very good-looking, in a wholesome, intelligent, capable sort of a way. Her name, Estra told them later, was Myrin; and he explained that he and she were associated solely because of their mutual interest in the same planet—the Earth.

Said Myrin: "You are accustomed to the idea of government. We, however, have outgrown it.

"If you stop to think, you will agree that the purpose of government is to maintain peace, on the one hand, and to wage war, on the other. Now, as to war—we haven't even separate nations, any more. So we have no wars. And as for internal conflict—why should we ever quarrel, when each of us is assured all that he can possibly want?"

"So you have abolished government?"

"A very long time ago. You on the earth will do the same, as soon as your people have been educated up to the point of trusting each other."

"You haven't even a congress, then?"

Myrin shook her head. "All questions such as a congress would deal with, were settled ages ago. You must remember that the material features of our civilization have not changed for thousands of generations. The only questions that come

114

up now are purely personal ones, which each must settle for himself."

Van Emmon, as before, was not at all satisfied. "You say that machinery does your work for you. I presume you do not mean that literally; there must be some duties which cannot be performed without human direction, at least. How do you get these duties accomplished, if you have no government to compel your people to do them?"

Myrin looked at a loss, either for the answer itself or for the most suitable words. Estra gave the reply: "Every device we possess is absolutely automatic. There is not one item in the materials we use but that was constructed, exactly as you see it now, many thousands of years ago."

Smith was incredulous. "Do you mean to say that those little glass pews have been in use all that time?"

Estra nodded, smiling gently at the engineer's amazement. "Like everything else, they were built to last. You must remember that we do not have anything like an 'investment,' here; we do not have to consider the question of 'getting our capital back.' So, if any further improvements were to be made, they also would be done in a permanent fashion."

Billie gave an exclamation of bewilderment. "I don't understand! You say that nothing new has been built, or even replaced, for centuries. How do you take care of your increase in population?" thinking of the great crowd that had just left.

Myrin was the one who answered this. As she did so, she got slowly to her feet; and speaking with the utmost care, watched to be sure that the four understood her:

"Ever since the roof was put on, our increase of population has been exactly balanced by our death rate!"

The four followed their guides in silence as they led the way into the plaza. Now, the space was alive with Venusians. The little cages were everywhere floating about in the air; some of the people were laboriously shifting themselves into their aircraft; others were guiding their "pews" direct to nearby houses. The visitors got plenty of curious stares from these quiet miracle-workers, who seemed vastly more at home

115

in the air than on the ground. "As thick as flies," Van Emmon commented.

Estra and Myrin, walking very slowly, took them to a side street, where two of the cigar-shaped cars were standing. Billie and Smith got in with Estra, while Van Emmon and the doctor were given seats beside the Venusian woman. The two cars were connected by telephone, so that in effect the two parties were one.

By this time, the visitors had become so accustomed to the transparent material that they felt no uneasiness as the ground receded below them. Smith, especially, was tremendously impressed with Estra's declaration that the glass was, except for appearance, nothing more nor less than an extremely strong, steel alloy.

Propelled by the unexplained forces which the two drivers controlled by means of buttons in black cases, the two cars began to thread their way through the great roof-columns; and as they proceeded, the four grew more and more amazed at the great extent of the city. For miles upon miles that heterogeneous collection of buildings stretched, unbroken and without system, until the eye tired of trying to make out the limits of it.

"What is the name of this city?" asked Billie, secretly hoping that it might bear some resemblance to "New York." It struck her fancy to assume that this supermetropolis represented what Gotham, in time, might become.

Estra did not take his attention from what he was doing, but answered as readily as ever. "I do not blame you for mistaking this for a city. The fact is, however, that we have no such thing."

Billie stared at him helplessly. "You've abolished cities, too?"

"Not exactly. In the same sense that we have abolished nations, yes. Likewise we have abolished states, also counties. Neither have we such a thing as 'the country,' now.

"My friends, Venus is simply one immense city."

116

IX

THE SURVIVAL OF ALL

SOMEHOW ALL FOUR were unwilling to press this question. It did not seem possible that Estra was right, or, if he was, that they could possibly understand his explanation, should he give it. The cars flew side by side for perhaps a hundred miles, while the visitors put in the time in examining the landscape with the never-ending interest of all aeronauts.

Here and there, in that closely-packed surface, a particularly large building was to be noted every half mile or so. "Factories?" asked Billie of Estra, but he shook his head.

"I'll show you factories later on," said he. "What you see are schools." But most observers would have considered the structures severely plain for their purpose.

After a long silence: "I'm still looking for streams," said Van Emmon to Myrin. "Are your rivers as large as ours?"

"We have no rivers," was the calm reply. "Rivers are entirely too wasteful of water. All our drainage is carried off through underground canals."

"You haven't done away with your oceans, too, have you?" the geologist asked, rather sarcastically. But he was scarcely prepared for the reply he got.

"No; we couldn't get along without them, I am afraid. However, we did the best we could in their case." And without signaling to Estra she dove the machine towards the ground. Smith looked for the telephone wires to snap, but Estra seemed to know, and instantly followed Myrin's lead. The doctor noticed, and wondered all the more.

And then came another surprise. As the machines neared the surface, a familiar odor floated in through the open windows of the air-craft; and the four found themselves looking at each other for signs of irrationality. A moment, and they saw that they were not mistaken.

For, although that kaleidoscopic expanse of buildings

117

showed not the slightest break, yet they were now located on the sea. The houses were packed as closely together as anywhere; apparently all were floating, yet not ten square yards of open sea could be seen in any one spot.

Van Emmon almost forgot his resentment in his growing wonder. "That gets me, Myrin! Those houses seem to be merely floating, yet I see no motion whatever! Why are there no waves?"

The doctor snorted. "Shame on you, Van! Don't let our friends think that you're an absolute ignoramus." He added: "Venus has no moon, and no wind, at least under the roof. Therefore, no waves."

Smith put in: "That being the case, there is no chance to start a wave-motor industry here. Neither," as he thought further, "neither for water-power. Having no rain in your mountains, Estra, where do you get your power?"

But it was Myrin who answered. "I suppose you are all familiar with radium? It is nothing more or less than condensed sunlight, which in turn is simply electromagnetic waves; although it may take your scientists a good many centuries to reach that conclusion.

"Well, every particle of the material which composes this planet, contains radioactivity of some sort; and we long ago discovered a way to release it and use it. One pound of solid granite yields enough energy to—well, a great deal of power."

They had now been flying for two hours, and still no end to that thickly-housed, ever different appearance of the ground. Also, although they saw a great many birds, they noted no animals. Finally, Billie could hold in no longer.

"Are we to understand," she demanded of Estra, "that the whole of this planet is as densely populated as we see it?"

"Just that," replied the Venusian. "Why not? The roof makes our climate uniform from pole to pole, while our buildings are such that, whether on land or on sea, they are equally livable."

"But—Estra!" expostulated the girl. "Venus is nearly as big as the earth. And it looks to be as thickly populated as—

as Rhode Island! Why, you must have a colossal population; let me see." And she scribbled away in her memorandum book.

But both Smith and the doctor had already worked it out. They looked up, blinking dazedly.

"Over three hundred billion," murmured the doctor, as though dizzy.

The Venusian checked Smith's correction with, "You dropped one cipher, doctor. There are three and a half trillion of us!"

"Good lord!" whispered Van Emmon, all his antagonism gone for the moment. And again the explorers were silent for a long time.

By and by, however—"We have just seen what it meant, there on Mercury," said the doctor, in a low voice, "for the principle of 'the survival of the fit' to be carried to its logical end; for who is to decide what is fitness, save the fittest? One man, apparently, outlived every one else on the planet, and then he also died.

"But here you have gone the limit in the other direction. Of course, we might have known that you long ago abolished poverty, unearned wealth, pestilence, drunkenness and the other causes of premature death; but as for three and a half trillion!"

"Nevertheless," remarked Myrin, "every last one of us, once born, lives to die of old age; and in most cases this means several hundred of your years."

Smith involuntarily rubbed his eyes; and they all laughed, a nervous sort of a laugh which left the visitors still in doubt as to their senses, and their guides' sanity. Van Emmon's suspicions came back with a rush, and he burst out:

"Say—you'll excuse me, but I can't swallow this! Here you've shown us houses as thick as leaves; not a sign of a farm, much less an orchard! No vegetation at all, except for a few flowers!

"Three and a half trillion! All right; let it go at that!" Out came his chin, and he brought one fist down upon the other

119

as though he were cracking rocks with a hammer, and with every blow he uttered a word:

"How—do—you—feed—them—all?"

X

LOAVES AND FISHES

WITHOUT A WORD Myrin drove her machine toward the ground, and, as before, Estra followed despite the lack of any visible signal. Within a minute the two machines had come to rest, softly and without disturbance, on the roof of a handsome building, much like an apartment house. There was the usual transparent elevator, and a minute later the four were being introduced to the occupants of a typical Venusian house.

These two people, apparently man and wife, did not need to be told why the explorers had been brought there. They led the way from the dimly lighted hallway in which the elevator had stopped, into a group of brightly decorated rooms. Here the four were given seats in the usual saddellike chairs, and then Myrin answered Van Emmon's question:

"I knew that this point would arise soon, and you will pardon me if I handle it in a prearranged fashion. I will admit that it is not an easy question Mr. Van Emmon has put; not because the answer is at all complicated but, on the contrary, extremely simple."

The four were listening unanimously. Despite himself, Van Emmon was highly impressed by the Venusian woman's serious manner. Perhaps it was because, in her earnestness, she was not quite so affable as before. She went on:

"From where you are sitting, you can see all the rooms in this house. You will look in vain for anything even remotely resembling a kitchen. There is not even a dining-room.

"And yet you must not jump to the conclusion that we all use restaurants. We have no such thing as a public eating place. Or rather," and here she spoke very carefully, "rather, every place is an eating place."

The doctor looked Myrin over as though she were a patient with a new kind of disease. "You do not mean that literally, of course," said he kindly.

But she nodded gravely. "You must not misunderstand. Remember, even on your own planet, the distribution of food is becoming more and more extensive, until you can now buy something to eat at every crossroads. We have merely carried the idea to its logical end, so that all Venusians can obtain food at any time, and at any spot."

She turned in her chair—all the chairs on Venus were pivoted, Estra said—and touched a button in the wall at her hand. A panel slid noiselessly aside, and revealed a tiny buffet. At least, Billie labeled it a buffet, for want of a more accurate term.

For it consisted of a silver bibb, something like the nozzle of a soda-water fountain above which was a board containing a large number of tiny, numbered push buttons. Below the bibb was a space in which a cup might be set, and projecting from a tube at one side was a solid block of telescoping, transparent cups.

"This," said Myrin, "is the Venusian Nutrition System. There is a station like this in every room on the planet." And she proceeded to take a cup from the tube, filling each from the silver faucet while she pressed a variety of the buttons.

The four watched in silence, and eagerly took what was given to them. It comprised liquids entirely; liquids of every degree of fluidity, from some as thin as water to others as thick as gruel. They varied even more as to color, ranging from actual transparency to a deep chocolate.

"Now, I warn you not to be shocked," said Myrin, "although I fully expect that you will be. The fact is that we have no other kind of food than what you see; there are thousands upon thousands of different kinds and flavors, but they are all fluids. We have nothing whatever in solid form.

"You see," she explained, "we have no teeth."

All they could do was to stare at her as, with a return of

121

her smile, she made a sudden gesture across the front of her mouth. Next instant a set of false teeth lay in her hand!

Estra spoke up. "We are both obliged to wear them in order that we might use your language." He removed his own, to show a mouth as free of teeth as a newborn baby's. Both Venusians replaced their sets, and smiled afresh at the explorers' astonishment.

"Teeth will soon be a thing of the past with you on the Earth, too," commented Myrin. "Dr. Kinney will surely testify to that. Your use of soft, cooked foods, instead of the coarse, hard articles provided by nature, is bound to have this effect in time. With us, it resulted in having teeth reduced to the standing of your appendix; and, like you, we resort to an operation rather than take chances on trouble. I may mention that the appendix is totally absent from all Venusians, while we are beginning to lose all traces of either the first or second molars; just as you are beginning to lose your wisdom teeth.

"However, suppose you try our diet while I explain."

The four once more looked at each other. The doctor was the first to take a sip of one of the cups handed to him, and Van Emmon was the last; the geologist waited to see the effects upon the others before gingerly tasting of the thickest, darkest liquid of them all. Another taste, and he discovered that it was very good, and that he was exceedingly hungry.

"Very delicately flavored," commented Billie, after emptying her fourth glass, a golden fluid with a slightly oily appearance.

"Delicately is right," said the doctor. "This stuff is barely flavored at all, Estra."

The Venusian was also "eating." "We much prefer them all that way," said he. "I suppose you would consider our tastes very finicky, on Earth; but the fact is we are able to distinguish between minute variations in flavoring such as would escape all on earth except a humming-bird."

"I suppose," remarked the doctor, smacking his lips over a reddish solution with a winelike flavor, "I suppose we can expect something of that sort on the Earth, too, in time.

Originally mankind was only able to distinguish fresh from stale, and animal from vegetable flavors."

After a while Myrin went on: "You know, the processes of nutrition, as they take place among your people, are extremely wasteful. You have probably heard it said that 'the average human is only fifty per cent efficient.' That simply means that digestion, assimilation and excretion require half the energy which they secure from the food.

"Now, the articles you have just swallowed require very little work on the part of your digestive apparatus, and none at all upon your eliminating tract. The food is almost instantly transformed into fresh blood; if I am not mistaken, you already feel much refreshed."

This was decidedly true. All four felt actually stimulated; Van Emmon instantly suspected the food of being alcoholic. As he continued to watch its effect, however, he saw that there was no harmful reaction as in the case of the notorious drug.

"I think I can now tell you how we produce enough food for the three and a half trillion of us, despite our lack of farms and orchards," said Myrin rising.

Returning to the air-craft, the four were taken a short distance in a new direction, and again descended, this time transferring to an elevator which dropped far below the surface. They came to a stop about ten floors down.

"Naturally," said Myrin, "we reserve all the surface for residence purposes; although, it is possible to live down here in comparative comfort, since we have plenty of electrical energy to spare." And she operated a switch, flooding the place with a brilliant glow. Thrown from concealed sources, this light was quite as strong as the subdued daylight which they had just left. "But unless we were free to fly about as much as we do, we should feel that life was a bore. Nobody stays below any longer than is necessary.

"Now, this is where our food comes from." Whereupon she showed them a series of automatic machines, all working away there in the solid rock of the planet; and of such an extraordinary nature that Smith, the engineer, moved about in an atmosphere of supreme bliss.

"You will understand," said Myrin, "that the usual processes of nutrition, on the Earth, depend entirely upon plant life. We, however, cannot spare room enough for any such system; so we had to devise substitutes for plants.

"In effect, that is what these machines are. They convert bed-rock into loam, take the nitrates and other chemicals* directly from this artificial soil, and by a pseudo-osmotic process secure results similar to those produced by roots.

"Likewise we have developed artificial leaves," pointing out a huge apparatus which none but a highly trained expert in both botany and mechanics could half understand. "This machine first manufactures chlorophyl—yes, it does," as the doctor snorted incredulously; "not an imitation, but real chlorophyl—and then transforms the various elements into starch, sugar, and proteids through the agency of the sunlight recovered from the granite.

"In short, to answer your question, Mr. Van Emmon, as to how we are all fed—we do not grow our food at all; we go straight to the practically unlimited supply of raw materials under our feet, and manufacture our food, outright!"

XI

THE SUPER-AMBITION

BILLIE WAS VERY quiet during their return to the surface. She said nothing until they had reached the two cars; and then pausing as she was about to step in, she said:

"Well, I never saw our old friend, the high cost of living, handled quite so easily!

"If that's the way you do things here, Estra," and the girl did not flinch at the gazes the others turned upon her, "if

---

*The geology of Venus is thoroughly described in Mr. Van Emmon's reports to the A. M. E. A.

that's your way, it's good enough for me! I'm going to stay!"

For the first time, Estra looked astonished. He and Myrin exchanged lightninglike glances; then the Venusian's face warmed with the smile he gave the architect.

"It is very good of you to say that," he said impressively. "I was afraid some of our—peculiarities—might arouse very different feelings."

They stared at one another for a second or two, long enough for the doctor to notice, and to see how Van Emmon took it. The geologist, however, was smiling upon the girl in a big-brotherly fashion, which indicated that he thought she didn't mean what she had said. Had he been looking up at her, however, instead of down upon her, he would have seen that her chin was most resolute.

Just as they were about to start again, both Estra and Myrin stopped short in their tracks, with that odd hesitation that had mystified the four all along; and after perhaps five seconds of silence turned to one another with grave faces. It was Estra who explained.

"It is curious how things do pile up," said he, a little conscious of having employed an idiom. "Our planet has gone along for hundreds of generations without anything especially remarkable happening, so that recently many prophets have foretold a number of startling events to take place on a single day. And this seems to have come true.

"You have been with us scarcely ten hours," and the visitors stared at each other in amazement that so much time had passed; "scarcely ten hours, and here comes an announcement which, for over a hundred years, has been looked forward to with—"

He stopped abruptly. The doctor gently took him up: " 'Looked forward to with'—what, Estra?"

Estra and Myrin considered this for perhaps three seconds. It was the woman who replied: "The fact is, your approach to the planet has stimulated all sorts of research immensely. Matters that had been hanging fire indefinitely were revived; this is one of them. In that sense, you are to blame." But she

125

smiled as reassuringly as she could, allowing for a certain anxiety which had now come to her face.

"Don't you think you could make it clear to us?" asked Billie encouragingly. At the same time all four noted that the air, which before had fairly thronged with machines, was now simply alive with them. People were flitting here and there like swarms of insects, and with as little apparent aim. Both Estra and Myrin were extra watchful; also, they displayed a certain eagerness to get away, setting their course in still another direction. In a minute or two the congestion seemed relieved, and Myrin began to talk slowly:

"You have doubtless guessed, by this time, that we Venusians have crossed what some call 'the animal divide.' We are predominatly intellectual, while you on the earth are, as a race, still predominantly animal. Excuse me for putting it so bluntly."

"It's all right," said the doctor, with an effort. "What you say is true—of most of us." He added: "Most thinking people realize that when our civilization reaches the point where the getting of a living becomes secondary, instead of primary as at present, a great change is bound to come to the race."

The Venusian nodded. "Under the conditions which now surround us, you can see, we have vastly more time for what you would call spiritual matters. Only, we label them psychological experiences.

"In fact, the 'supernatural' is the Venusian's daily business!"

There was another pause, during which both Venusians, driving at high speed though they were, once more closed their eyes for a second or so. Estra evidently thought it time to explain.

"For instance, 'telepathy.' With us it takes the place of wireless; for we have developed the power to such a point that any Venusian can 'call up' any other, no matter where either may be. That is why we need no signs or addresses. There are certain restrictions; for instance, no one can read another's thoughts without his permission. Of course, we still have speech; speech and language are the ABC's of the Venusian; and we still keep the telephone, for the sake of checking up now and then. Just now, we are driving for my own house, where there is apparatus which will enable you to both hear and understand an announcement which is shortly to be made."

There was something decidedly satisfying, especially to Van Emmon, in being taken into the Venusian confidence to this extent. When he put his question, it was with his former aggressiveness much modified. He said:

"I should think that your people have pretty well exhausted the possibilities of the supernatural, by this time. Progress having come to an end, I don't see what you find to interest you, Myrin."

"The fact is," Billie put in, "we feel somewhat disappointed that your people have shown so little interest in us." And she gave a sidelong glance at Estra, who returned the look with a direct, smiling gaze which sent a flood of color into the architect's face.

"Look out!" sharply, from Van Emmon; and with barely an inch to spare, Estra steered his car past another which he had nearly overlooked. For another minute or two there was silence; then Myrin said:

"You wonder what there is to interest us. And yet, every time you look up at the stars, the answer is before your eyes.

"You see, although we cannot read your thoughts without your permission, yet you on the earth cannot prevent us from 'overhearing' anything that may be said. Under proper conditions, our psychic senses are delicate enough to feel the slightest whisper on the earth.

"That is why Estra and I are able to use your language; we have learned it together with an understanding of your lives and customs, by simply 'listening in.' I may add that we are also able to use your eyes; we knew, directly, what you people looked like before you arrived.

"Well, it is our ambition to visit, in spirit, every planet in the universe!

"There are hundreds of millions of stars; every one is a sun; and each has planets. One in a hundred contains life; some very elementary, others much more advanced than we are.

THE QUEEN OF LIFE

"So far, we have been able to study nearly two thousand worlds besides those in this solar system. Do you still think, friend, we have nothing to interest us?"

She raised a hand in a gesture of emphasis; and it was then that Billie, her eyes on Myrin's fingers, saw another sign of the great advancement these people had made—direct proof, in fact, of what Myrin had just claimed.

For there must have been a tremendous gain in the intellect to have caused such a drain upon the body as Billie saw. Li no other way could it be explained; the minds of the Venusians had grown at a fearful cost to flesh and blood.

Not only were the fingernails entirely lacking from Myrin's hand, but the lower joints of her four fingers, from the palm to the knuckles were grown smoothly together.

XII

THE MENTAL LIMIT

"Make yourselves at home," said Estra, as they stepped into his apartment. The cars just filled his balcony. "This is my 'workshop'; see if you can guess my occupation, from what you see. As for Myrin and myself, we must make certain preparations before the announcement is made."

They disappeared, and the four inspected the place. As in the other house they had entered, the room was provided with a double row of small windows; some being down near the floor and the others level with the eyes. These, in addition to two doors, all of which were of translucent material.

On low benches about the room were a number of instruments, some of which looked familiar to the doctor. He said he had seen something much like them in psychology class, during his college days. For the most part, their appearance defied ordinary description.*

---

*Physicians, biologists, and others interested in matters of this nature will find the above fully treated in Dr. Kinney's reports to the A. M. A.

But one piece of apparatus was given such prominence that it is worth detailing. It consisted of a hollow, cube-shaped metal framework; about a foot in either direction, upon which was mounted about forty long thumb-screws, all pointing toward the inside of the frame. The inner ends of the screws were provided with small silver pads; while the outer ends were so connected, each with a tiny dial, as to register the amount of motion of the screw. Smith turned one of them in and out, and said it reminded him of a micrometer gage.

Then Billie noted that the entire device was so placed upon the bench as to set directly over a hole, about ten inches in diameter. And under the bench was one of the saddlelike chairs. The architect's antiquarian lore came back to her with a rush, and she remembered something she had seen in a museum—a relic of the inquisition.

"Good Heavens!" she whispered. "What is this—an instrument of torture?"

It certainly looked mightily like one of the head-crushing devices Billie had seen. Thumb-screws and all, this appeared to be only a very elaborate "persuader," for use upon those who must be made to talk.

But the doctor was thinking hard. A big light flashed into his eyes. "This," he declared, positively, "is something that will become a matter of course in our own educational system, as soon as the science of phrenology is better understood." And next second he had ducked under the bench, and thrust his head through the round hole, so that his skull was brought into contact with some of those padded thumb-screws.

"Get the idea?" he finished. "It's a cranium-meter!"

It did not take Smith long to reach the next conclusion. "Then," said he, "our friend Estra is connected with their school system. Can't say what he would be called, but I should say his function is to measure the capacity of students for various kinds of knowledge, in order that their education may be adapted accordingly.

"Might call him a brain-surveyor," he concluded.

"Or a noodle-smith," added the geologist, deprecatingly.

"Rather, a career-appraiser!" indignantly, from Billie. "People look to him to suggest what they should take up, and what they should leave alone. Why, he's one of the most important men on this whole planet!"

And again the doctor was a witness to a clash of eyes between the girl and the geologist. Van Emmon said nothing further, however, but turned to examine an immense bookcase on the other side of the room.

This case had shelves scarcely two inches apart, and about half as deep, and held perhaps half a million extremely small books. Each comprised many hundreds of pages, made of a perfectly opaque, bluish-white material of such incredible thinness that ordinary India-paper resembled cardboard by comparison.

They were printed much the same as any other book, except that the characters were of microscopic size, and the lines extremely close together. Also, in some of the books these lines were black and red, alternating.

Billie eagerly examined one of the diminutive volumes under a strong glass, and pronounced the black-printed characters not unlike ancient Gothic type. She guessed that the language was synthetic, like Roman or Esperanto, and that the alphabet numbered sixty or seventy.

"The red lines," she added, not so confidently, "are in a different language. Looks wonderfully like Persian." By this time the others were doing the same as she, and marveling to note that, wherever the red and black lines were employed, invariably the black were in the same language; while the red characters were totally different in each book.

Suddenly Smith gave a start, so vigorously that the other turned in alarm. He was holding one of the books as though it were white hot. "Look!" he stuttered excitedly. "Just look at it!"

And no wonder. In the book he had chanced to pick up, the red lines were printed in *English*.

"Talk about your finds!" exclaimed Billie, in an awe-struck tone. "Why, this library is a literal translation of the lan-

guages of"—she fairly gasped as she recalled Myrin's words
—"thousands of planets!"

After that she fell silent. Plainly the discovery had pro-
foundly affected and strengthened her notion of remaining
on the planet. Van Emmon, watching her narrowly, saw her
give the room an appraising glance which meant, plain as
day, "I'd like to keep this place in spick and span condition!"
And another, not so easy to interpret: "I'd like to show these
people a thing or two about designing houses!" And the
geologist's heart sank for an instant. .

He turned resolutely to the bookcase, and shortly found
something which he showed to the doctor. It was a book
printed all in "Venusian." They carefully translated the
title-page, using one of the interlinear English books as a
guide; and saw that it was a complete text-book on astral
development.

"With these instructions," the doctor declared, "any one
could do as the Venusians do—visit other worlds in spirit!"

Just then Estra and Myrin returned. They were moving at
what was, for them, a rapid pace; and to all appearances
they were rather excited.

"We were not able to make these records as perfect as
we would like," said Estra, holding up four disks similar to
the ones which still lay in the explorers' translating machines.
He proceeded to open the little black cases and make the
exchange. "There will be words used which I did not see fit
to incorporate in the original vocabulary, but which you will
have to understand perfectly if this announcement is to mean
anything to you."

"Thank you," said the doctor quietly. "And now, don't you
think we had best know in advance, just what is to be the
subject of—"

"Hush!" whispered Estra; and next second they were listening to the telephone in amazement.

XIII

THE WAR OF THE SEXES

"In accordance with my promise," stated a high-pitched effeminate voice, "I am going to demonstrate a juvenation method upon which I have worked for the past one hundred and twenty-two years."

There was a brief pause, during which Estra hurriedly explained that the man who was making the speech was located far on the other side of the planet, in a hall like the one the four had first visited; and that he was making the demonstration before a great gathering of scientists. "Too bad you cannot see as we do," commented the Venusian. "However, Savarona may go into the details of—"

"If the committeemen are entirely finished with their measurements," stated the unseen experimenter, "I would like to have the results compared with the recorded figures of Pario Camenol, who was born on the two hundred and fifteenth day of the year twenty-one thousand seven hundred and four."

Another rest, and Estra said: "They are examining a boy who appears to be about twelve years of age."

Then came other voices: "As we all know, the craniums of us all are absolutely distinct; as much so as our finger-prints." "The measurements correspond identically with those of Pario Camenol, beyond a doubt." "This boy can be none other than Pario."

"Then," the high-pitched voice went on, "then notice the formula I have written on this blackboard. Using this solution, I have supplied nourishment to this lad from the hour of his birth. Until a few days ago, I was not satisfied with the results; the patient showed a tiny variation from the allowable subconscious maximum, together with only nine-tenths the required motor reaction.

"But I have corrected this. Briefly, I have incorporated in

Pario Camenol's standard diet certain elements which have hitherto been unsafe to combine. These elements are derivatives of the potash group, for the most part, together with phosphates which need a new classification. Their effect," impressively, "has been to postpone age indefinitely!"

There must have been a tremendous sensation in that hall. The speaker's voice shook with excitement as he went on:

"We have sought in vain, friends, for a way to cheat death of his due. We have succeeded in postponing his advent until our average longevity is several times greater than on our neighboring planet. But so far, it has been a mere reprieve.

"What I have done is to prevent age itself. This lad is a hundred and twenty-two years old, mentally, and still only twelve years old, as to body!

"In short, I offer you the fountain of youth itself!"

The speaker paused. There was no comment. Evidently all had been as greatly impressed as the explorers. Then the voice of the man Savarona finished, very deliberately:

"I regret to say that my treatment, despite all that I have been able to do, cannot be adapted to the female constitution. It would be fatal to any but males. I repeat—I can offer eternal youth, absolutely, but only to new-born males!"

This time there was a definite response. From the telephone came a confused murmuring, at which Van Emmon's face lighted up with delight. The murmuring had an angry sound!

"This is outrageous!" a loud contralto voice was raised above the rest. "You are unethical, Savarona, to announce such a thing before adapting it to both sexes!"

The high-pitched voice replied shortly, and with more than a hint of malice: "If a woman had discovered this, instead of me, I dare say you would have no objections!"

The murmuring grew louder, angrier, more confused. The four from the earth looked at each other in some slight uneasiness. At the same time they noted that Estra, his eyes tightly closed and his fists clenched in the intensity of his concentration, suddenly gave a sigh of relief. Next second he began to speak into the telephone, in a voice so loud as to silence all the clamor.

"Savarona, and the people of Venus! Listen!

"The prophets were right when they said today would witness many great things! I have just learned of another experiment which transcends even that of Savarona!"

An instant's pause; then: "First let me remind you that we have been doing all we could to elevate our spiritual selves. We are daily trying to eliminate all that is animal, all that is gross and bemeaning in us, even to the extent of reducing the flavors of our foods to the lowest tolerable point. And despite all this, we have not been able to get rid of sex jealousy!

"We still have the beast within us! No matter how pure our love may be, it is always tainted with rivalry! Always the husband and wife are held down by this mutual envy, forever dragging at their heels, constantly holding them back from the lofty heights of spiritual power to which they aspire!"

He paused, and Savarona's voice broke in, triumphantly: "You are right, Estra! You are right, except you did not mention that this jealousy becomes less and less as one grows older!

"Now, my discovery will put an end to your beast, Estra! My experiments took this lad before he had become a man, and allowed his brain to develop, while his body stopped growing! He is a man in mentality, and an innocent boy in body!

"Estra, I have done the thing you wish! This boy will never know jealousy, because he will never know love!"

The man in the room with the four answered in a flash: "So you have, Savarona, but only for *men!* No female can benefit by what you have done!

"But I tell you that, within the past few minutes, a child has been born under circumstances which can be repeated at any time, and for any sex!

"In this case," the Venusian's voice changed curiously; "in this case, however, it was a girl; for the mother controlled the sex in the customary manner." At this, the doctor's interest became acute. At the same time, the other three felt a tremendous, inexplicable thrill.

"Friends"—and Estra's face shone in his enthusiasm—"friends, for the first time in creation the human male germ has been dispensed with! The intellect has done what the laboratory could not do!

"I have the honor to announce that my sister, Amra, has just given birth"—his voice fairly rang—"has just given birth to a girl baby, whose only father was her mother's brain!"

XIV

ESTRA

THIS TIME there was no drowning the confusion. The telephone fairly shook with innumerable cries, shouts, imprecations. The four gave up trying to hear, and watched the two Venusians.

Myrin was facing Estra now. Her expression had lost a great deal of its good humor, and there was a certain sharpness in her voice as she exclaimed:

"Estra—if your sister has done this, and I see no reason to doubt it, then she has made man superfluous! If women can produce children mechanically, and govern the sex at will, the coming race need be nothing but females!"

Estra nodded gravely. "That is what it amounts to, Myrin!"

For a moment the two stared at one another challengingly. On the earth, their attitude would have indicated some unimportant tiff. None would have dreamed that the most momentous question in their lives had come up, and had found them at outs.

Next instant Myrin turned, and without another word walked from the room. Estra followed slowly to the door, where he stood looking after her with an expression of the keenest concern on his sensitive, high-strung features. The three men from the earth, after a glance, studiously avoided looking at him; but Billie walked up and laid a hand on his arm.

"Are you really in favor of this—scheme?" she inquired, in a curiously tender voice. At the same time she gazed intently into Estra's eyes.

He turned, and the smile came back to his face. He took Billie's hand and laid it between both his own. His voice was even gentler than before.

"Most certainly I do favor my sister's method, Billie. It will be the greatest boon the race has ever known. We can look forward, now"—and his face shone again—"can look forward to generation upon generation of people whose spirituality will be absolute!"

The girl moved closer to him. She spoke with feverish earnestness.

"There may be some hitch in the idea, Estra. If God meant for man to become—to become obsolete, He would not have hidden the method all this time. Suppose some flaw should develop—later on?"

In the cube, Billie Jackson would not have stumbled over such a speech. She would have ignored the fact that Estra was holding her hand all this time, and gazing deep into her eyes; she would have been filled with what she was saying and not with what she was seeing. On the other side of the room, Van Emmon watched and glowered; he could not hear.

The Venusian lifted his head suddenly. The voices from the telephone had subsided; only an occasional outburst came from the instrument. Estra closed his eyes again for a second, and when he opened them again, his manner was astonishingly alert, and his speech swift and to the point.

"So far as we know, Billie, the method has no flaws. It gives us the chance to throw off our lower selves; and if by so doing, we reduce the race to a single sex, only—"

He stopped short, as though at a sound; and with a word of apology stepped from the room. He opened another door, far down the corridor; and as he passed through, the wail of a new-born infant came faintly to the four.

"Wonder what's up?" said Smith. Van Emmon, who had

gone to the window, whirled upon the engineer and motioned him to his side.

"Look at the people!"

Smith saw that the nearby houses were almost concealed by a throng which had gathered, silently and without confusion, during the past few minutes. Their numbers were increasing swiftly, fresh arrivals packing the background. People filled the streets; the space below Estra's balcony was already crowded as closely as it could be. Except for a low-voiced buzzing, there was no disturbance.

Billie came up. She seemed to divine the temper of the mob. She caught her breath sharply, and then said, very simply:

"It reminds me of—Bethlehem."

But the words had scarcely left her mouth before an uproar sounded from one end of the street below. A crowd of excited Venusians was pushing its way determinedly toward the house, their passage obstructed by shouting, protesting individuals. Van Emmon's breast began to heave; he fancied he saw blows struck.

"By George!" he exclaimed, next second. "They're fighting!"

It was true; a hand-to-hand battle was going on less than a block away. The people below the window surged in the direction of the fight; all were shouting, now; the clamor was deafening.

"Live and let live!" came one of the shouts. It was taken up by the group that was doing the attacking, and made into a cheer. Then came other cries from them. Smith made out something like "Down with sex monopoly!"

"Don't you see?" shouted Smith, above the din. "These people below are Estra's friends; those newcomers are backing Savarona! Get the idea?" he repeated. "If Estra wins out, the old boy with the fountain of youth will never get another boy baby to experiment on!"

"What!" The doctor leaped to their sides. He took it in at a glance; then whirled to the door. "We ought to warn Estra!"

"He knows it already!" reminded Billie swiftly. A great shout came from below; the attackers had forced their way through the crowd of Estra's friends.

"Well!" Van Emmon stood squarely in the middle of the room. "So far as I'm concerned, Estra and his sister can face that crowd alone! I don't approve of the scheme!"

The doctor eyed him thoughtfully. "I'm not so sure, Van. This is a tremendous thing; we ought to—"

"Van is—right!" exploded Billie. Her voice rose to a shriek as a crash shook the house.

Next instant Myrin, for once in a hurry, broke into the room. She glanced about, missed Estra, looked slightly puzzled, and then frowned angrily as the Venusian himself stepped in. "You fooled me!" she shot at him. But he smiled apologetically. He was carrying a large package of leaflets, closely printed in Venusian; there seemed to be several thousand in the lot. He said, by way of explanation:

"I had to get ready. Savarona's people will be here any moment; they have destroyed the elevator, and—"

A wave of clamor burst from below. "They've broken the barrier," remarked Estra calmly; he turned to the door, then whirled at a crash which sounded from above. "Through the roof," he added. He did not even glance at the balcony, where the two cars barred the way against any attack from that direction.

Next second he again quit the room. Myrin hesitated a moment, irresolute, and then followed him thoughtfully. They never saw her again. As for Estra, he came back in a moment carrying a small, white bundle, which stirred in his arms. He unhesitatingly handed the child to Billie. His mouth moved soundlessly as a muffled shriek arose from the other end of the corridor; there was a thud, a metallic crash, and a great roar of voices. The mob had broken in, and up, through the back of the house. The first of the attackers thrust his head and shoulders into sight not ten feet away.

Estra touched something with his foot, and a door shot across the corridor. There was an instant's silence; then, the thunder of the mob, hurling itself against the door. The people were fairly snarling now. Estra closed the inner door.

"Estra!" shrilly, from Billie. She laid the baby down, and strode to the Venusian. "Let's get out of here! The car's on the balcony; nobody's in the way to interfere! Why not—"

A grinding, ripping jar from above, and Estra shook his head. The smile was gone, and his mouth was set and grim. "They'd catch us before we went a mile," he said, glancing at the infant, who had begun to cry, in a stifled, gasping way that tore at the nerves.

"Estra!" Billie pleaded; but he turned away. The doctor strode up to him and gripped his shoulder.

"What's the good, Estra? What can you accomplish even if you—"

The Venusian tapped his forehead. "I can *tell!*" he exclaimed, with a return of that exalted flush. "Just give me a chance to offer my sister's discovery to the world, and I shall be satisfied!" He touched the package of leaflets. "These are not written as clearly as they should be; but if I cannot hold them back, then these"—fingering the papers—"these go to the friends down below!" He moved closer to the window, but his eyes were on the door.

A rending crash told that the corridor was now open to the mob. There was a rush, and then the storm of the people battering the last door.

"Van! Doc! Billie!" Smith had the window open, and was stepping into one of the cars. Kinney and the geologist were at his side in an instant. The girl held back.

"Estra!" she begged. She picked up the baby, and with her free hand tugged at the Venusian's arm. "Come on! Don't sacrifice yourself!"

The door bulged under the attack. The noise was ear-splitting. Nevertheless Estra heard, and shook his head without looking at the woman from the Earth. She dashed to the window, then came back. "Hurry! There's a chance!" He stood unmoved, watchful and ready. "Estra! I want you to come!" Her face flamed. "Can't you see? Can't you see that

I—I want you?" She gasped as the door shrieked under the strain. "Come—if you're a man!"

The Venusian's face changed. He turned, and stared at the girl with eyes that held nothing but blank amazement. The grimness left his mouth, his lips partly opened. He took a step forward and threw an arm about her shoulders.

"Billie—I'm sorry! I never thought!" A crack showed at the edge of the door, and a roar smote their ears. Estra backed to the window. "Go!" he shouted. "Go quickly, while you can!"

Billie stood stock still, gazing at him. "I'm going to stay!" she screamed. "I'll take my chances with—"

He thrust her through the window. "You don't understand!" he shouted, and took the baby away from her, despite all her strength. Then a wonderfully tender light came into his eyes. He gripped Billie's hands, and spoke sorrowfully:

"Billie—I'm not what you thought! I'm not a man—I'm a woman!"

XV

BACK!

By the time Smith had driven the strange craft fifty yards, he had it under control. Billie glanced back; Estra was out on the balcony, now, and the mob was surging against the windows she had locked against them. She shifted the baby to the hollow of one arm while with the other she broke the cord of the packet.

At the sight, the crowd in the street gave voice. "Let us have it!" they were crying; they drowned out the uproar within the house. Estra did not even look at the other car.

Then the windows gave way. Like the breaking of a dam, a flood of Venusians poured and tumbled at Estra's feet. She raised her hand, and shouted something Billie could not hear; then, scarcely without pause, the crowd bore down upon her.

140

And even as she was crushed against the railing, with one hand she dropped the baby to eager, upstretched arms below; and with the other she tossed the package high in the air. There it broke apart, the air caught it, and the thousands of leaflets fluttered down upon that street full of sympathizers.

Leaflets, each of which described a discovery which was to give to women the power of abolishing the opposite sex, of making Venus a world not only one in country, one in industry and one in thought, but—one in sex!

The thunderous meaning of Estra's last action almost made Billie forget that it was, in truth, the woman's last act. For next moment her lifeless form was being crushed beneath the feet of that supremely cultured, marvelously civilized mob; for it was only a mob, despite its astounding advancement; a mob which had retained all the brute's fanaticism, and all the male jealousy of the female.

For they were all men.

The four had been on Venus almost twenty-four hours when Smith, knowing the condition of the machinery in the cube, warned the others that they must return. Secretly, he was tired of the Venusians' continual smiling; for they had fairly outdone each other to show the visitors all that could be shown. But it was Van Emmon who thought to ask for Estra's wonderful library.

"These chemicals and metals you are giving us," he said, making a regular speech of it, "are extremely welcome; they will enable us to perform experiments otherwise out of our reach.

"But Estra's books will mean still more to the people of the earth. If there is no one else with more need for them, who is going to put in a claim, then why not let us have them?"

Apparently the Venusians did not like the idea very well. "They must have thought it was like letting a monkey play with a rifle," the doctor afterward put it. But, for lack of a leader with any motive for objecting, and because Estra had

141

no living relatives to claim the library, somehow that incredible collection of intellectual gems got into the possession of the four. Nothing was said about it during the quiet leave-taking, and when the cube finally rose away from the roof, Van Emmon's face beamed with happiness and a great sigh of satisfaction escaped him.

"Well"—looking at the books—"they kind of make up for the fact that the folks didn't ask us to call again!"

And he turned and went straight to the kitchenette, where he proceeded with great speed and efficiency to set out the following:

Canned Soup.

Canned baked beans.   Fried bacon and egg.

Coffee.   Peaches.

"Come and get it!" he shouted. The doctor tore himself away from the books; Smith crawled out from the beloved machines; Billie came out shortly from her cubby-hole, and slipped into her seat in a highly excited manner. There was a brightness in her cheeks, and a noticeable change in her usually assured manner. This timidity, so utterly new to ·the girl, seemed most pronounced whenever Van Emmon chanced to look at her; which was quite often.

All four were ravenous. They had been away from the cube a day and a night, and "all we had to eat was something to drink," as Smith complained. Nothing whatever was said except "Please pass that" and "Thanks," for fully fifteen minutes.

At last they were satisfied. The doctor went back to the books; Smith returned to his oil-can and wrench. But Billie stood by the table, and began helping Van Emmon to clear up. In a moment they were face to face.

"Van," she said softly, and looked up at him wistfully. "Van—do you like me better this way?" Her eyes were almost piteous.

Into the man's face there came a look of amazement, followed by one of admiration, and another of genuine delight. He gave a little laugh, and unconsciously threw out his hands.

"Much better, Billie." Neither of them cared a particle whether Smith or the doctor saw that Billie, very simply and naturally, walked right into Van Emmon's arms. "Much better. Besides, you're really too graceful to wear anything else."